This is a work of fiction. The characters, incidents and dialogues in this book are of the author's imagination and are not to be construed as real. Any resemblance to actual events or persons, living or dead, is completely coincidental.

No part of this book may be reproduced or transmitted in any form or by any means, electronic or mechanical, including photocopying, recording, or by any information storage and retrieval system, without permission in writing from the publisher.

Copyright Anthology 2017
ISBN:
Published 31/03/2019
Cover Art by Pam Hage

Dedication

This anthology goes out to those who struggle on without reward...

Index

The Flight of the Newar by River Daniel - p.4

The Beginning: Edge of War by R.Malak – p.21

The Bone Witch by H.M.R Leeper – p.40

The Unwanted Presence by Arete B. Rogers – p.60

Phantoms at Glenkos by Matty Hughes – p.76

A Many-Faced Memory by Kathryn Solly – p.82

Wireless Connection by Billy Brinkley – p.94

The Way of Water by Pam Hage – p.115

Night Faces by Robert Richmond – p.135

Willie's Bad Day by Robert Richmond – p.159

The Flight of the Newar:
By River Daniel

    The night, silent and unmoving, was illuminated by glistening white pillars filled from root to stem with a bright magical light. The sky above was a blanket of darkness, leaving the town empty and devoid of all life. It was a perfect spot for romantic strolls and business that required the cover of darkness for its transactions. Without a cloud in sight the moon set out casting its ethereal glow upon the world below, leaving the rough and grey-bricked roads paved in silver.

    There was one street in particular that was set apart from the rest; away from the hustle and bustle of the marketplace on one side and the groans, shrieks and clattering metal of the factories on the other. It sat in between them like a gatekeeper between two different worlds. During the day the street was filled with noise and general industry, but during the darkness of night it provided a sense of peace and security that few could find in such an industrious town. The position of the street made it a welcome spot for those who could not afford much.

    It was inside one of these inns, with only candlelight through a window announcing its existence, that small black gloves ran a whetstone along a shining blade with a simple black leather handle. The blade's metal reflected the candlelight across the walls, making the room lighter and airier than it otherwise should be.

    The stone slid along the sword before finishing with a slow clink when it hit the blade's end. After hours of the silent, repetitive work, the black-clothed figure's smooth and sweeping routine was interrupted by a knocking on the door. Three quick taps echoed quietly around the small, sparse room as the figure failed to look up from the whetstone.

"Enter," the figure said in a gentle, lilting voice as she continued to sharpen her sword, taking no notice of the large form that had just entered the room. She lifted her head up, content she didn't need to remain in the shadow of the room now that her companion had returned. Mousy brown hair tumbled down to her shoulders, covering her dainty ears and settling around her neck, leaving her plump mouth and large brown eyes exposed.

"Your voice is getting better, Lillith," the voice boomed. Lillith shot him a toothed, hungry smile. She'd been practising her part for months now. It was about time she improved.

The hulking beast that entered just barely passed for a man, towering over the girl by at least two feet. His smile resembled an animal, as though sizing up the prey it was preparing to snatch up and devour. He'd clearly never mastered the art of smiling.

Lillith smiled up at him as he entered before turning back to her blade. "Any new leads, Gairn?" she asked in her best business-like tone, tough to do due to her small stature. For his part, Gairn walked passed her in silence, completely ignored the question and went to peer out of the window instead. There were two jugs of foaming liquid set on the sill, warm ale that had been left for them by Kas. Lillith always found her child's taste buds made the ale taste more unpleasant and bitter than it should, so she stayed away from the stuff until her body matured enough to enjoy the taste.

Gairn picked up the first metal jug though he made it look more like a teacup from a playset in his bearlike hands. He threw it back with a quick gulp, not even registering the sensation of the warm liquid or its taste. He picked up the second jug and drank it more slowly, peering out of the window as he drank in silence; as though he could make out the world going by through its smeary, grease-stricken pane. The girl watched him for a time before she sighed with boredom and returned to routinely sharpening her blade, mindful of wearing it down too much with the stone.

"You know, Gairn, you're too nice to the help. Kas only smiles at me patronisingly when I tell him to clean. At least when you tell him to do something you can 'assert' yourself a little more." She did her best to speak lightly, trying to show she was joking. Gairn didn't look away from the window or give any sign that he was listening to her, so Lillith stayed silent until it built to something uncomfortable.

For a time, that's how they stayed; Gairn staring out of the window with his now empty jug of ale and Lillith sharpening the shining blade with satisfaction. After it felt as though the silence went from mutual to angry Gairn whirled around, jug still in hand, to face her.

"Do you plan on doing ANY searching yourself? It doesn't matter how many times I go out, no children are going to speak to a beast of a man! I'm running out of time and you're still sat there. You have the looks and voice of a child which leaves you with no excuses now!" Lillith tuned out Gairn's ranting; it had become commonplace the last few days as he became more and more desperate for a new body. He took a step closer to her so she turned to listen with disinterest, laying her blade on the table as she did so. "You sit there all day and all night, wasting candles as though they aren't expensive enough, sharpening your blades until the shine's gone and muttering to yourself like a lunatic when I'm not around." She paid more attention at the final statement making him smile condescendingly. "These walls are thin and the neighbours hear everything that the 'strange girl next door' says. As if there isn't enough attention on us already, even in our own home our neighbours know there is something wrong."

The girl sighed inwardly before lifting her palm to silence Gairn. Lillith suddenly bared her teeth and curved her lips at the side as she stared at him. It looked inhuman, both hungry and aggressive, not that of an innocent child. Gairn's eyes narrowed and he took a step back at the perceived aggression before realising that the girl was trying to smile. She went back to a plain face as soon as he realised.

"Gairn, never forget who the superior in this relationship is, we're Newar. Appearances can be deceiving." Lillith took a breath and then looked down, suddenly insecure, "But, this is why I can't go out, not like this, not when I can't even smile like a human. More and more Newar are popping up than ever before which means more children are disappearing from towns and cities. People are suspicious of any child not acting as they should. So, if I go out I need to seem perfectly innocent and like any other kid if I don't want to be shackled and sent to the factories. As for the blade, well, it won't be long before we are discovered which means we'll need to be able to protect ourselves."

She tried smiling to Gairn again, making it more genuine, avoiding baring her teeth. It was far more convincing of a child that didn't often smile. Gairn watched to see the improvement before turning back to the window.

"I'm sorry," he said it quickly in a gruff, deep voice just loud enough for the girl to hear him. She sniffed and rubbed her nose delicately, afraid she would break it if she rubbed too hard.

He was only being so argumentative because his body was dying which was easily the most irritating thing about human bodies. They were fragile and couldn't handle the magic of the Newar inside them which made them grow and advance too quickly until they break down under the weight of the Newar. It was one of the many reasons that children were such good targets to take over. Gairn had control of his current body for three months, it was the body of a toddler when they took it; a far cry from the hulking behemoth that now stood before her. If they didn't find a body soon then it would be only a matter of time before Gairn broke down and returned to his original form of a demon. It would make going outside impossible for him. He'd be found and made to work until he dropped, forging weapons for the squads to hunt his own kind with.

It was frustrating for both of them.

As they settled in their own thoughtful silence Lillith couldn't help but make her eyes wander the room. Checking its corners and walls for cracks and lidless eyes as amber danced around from the flickering candle. While she watched the temperature dropped considerably and she felt her stretching flesh break out with goosebumps all over. Then, within this cold Lillith watched Gairn rub his arms with discomfort before the candle wick died, plunging them into darkness. Gairn cursed in frustration and Lillith searched the draws in the desk for a tinderbox, hands shaking as she did so. Finally she found it and, in mere moments, set the candle back alight and filled the small space with amber once more.

Maintaining the silence, Lillith now eyed the candle as it flickered and glowed. Their silence and thoughts were interrupted by a quiet knocking at the door and Lillith looked up to Gairn in fear immediately. She stowed the blade under her worktable and shrank down, doing her best to seem like a shy child, while Gairn stood up and paced towards the door, looking as stern as possible. He balled one hand into a fist, ready to slam into the first sign of a threat. He opened it quickly and the girl shuddered as there was a moment of silence before Gairn chuckled slightly.

"You scared us, boy!" he said with obvious humour. Lillith looked up as a tall, thin and timid boy entered. He wore the same dirty cleaner's garments he'd worn everyday for three months now, and his face held the same look of naïve innocence. The boy rarely spoke and, when he did, she didn't bother taking the time to listen. He never spoke sense and hadn't even noticed Gairn's ridiculous growth over the course of three months. The girl was convinced he was a fool, if not worse.

"Good ale, sir?" The boy spoke fast and in mutters, as though talking to himself as he picked up the two ale jugs and looked around the room quickly surveying the mess and concluding there was nothing worth paying immediate attention to.

"Refreshing as always, Kasap." Gairn spoke gruffly to the boy, keen for him to leave.

"Just call me Kas, sir, I forget the name Kasap."

Gairn only laughed in reply and the boy laughed along, as though joining Gairn in mocking him.

Stillness consumed the room and Lillith shuffled her feet awkwardly as Kas turned to leave the room, Gairn shot him a look hot with anger at being interrupted, though.

Lillith could have sworn she saw a hint of paranoia in his piercing eyes. Behind him, Lillith retrieved her sword and went back to sharpening the blade before speaking absentmindedly, "I'll go tomorrow so you just stay here okay? You need a new body, so I'll stop hiding out and put mine to good use. Maybe I'll see if I can get into one of the factories. Children disappear all the time down there so one more going missing won't raise suspicion." As soon as the words left her mouth she scolded herself silently knowing that no good could come of this, but she didn't stop herself saying any of it. Lillith didn't know why she said she'd go, she only had one rule as a Newar and that was 'self- preservation'.

Gairn stared at her, searching for doubt, before slowly nodding his assent. "Okay, in that case, I'll work on soundproofing the room a little while you're gone." Lillith smiled and lowered the sharpening stone. In the brief quiet she finally appraised the blade she'd been working on. It started as a weak, rusted piece of metal she bought for a tiny amount of copper coins to take off of a merchants hands though she most likely still overpaid for it. Now, after days endlessly cleaning, then sharpening the weapon it was finally ready for use. Lillith ran her hand along the blade's edge, feeling it thrum and react to her as she poured her magic into it. The leather of the hilt had streaks of red running through it; and various carvings, molten orange in colour, appeared all along the shining blade: enchantments, spells and seals of power. The sum of her inner magic and knowledge. She walked across to the small wooden wardrobe on the other side of the room and placed the sword inside it, next to four identical blades. The blades represented another reason why young children were perfect targets as they had pools of untapped magic that they hadn't learnt to use yet, perfect for a Newar to store away then tap into, just as the girl had done with her collection. Usually it took two or more bodies to fill a blade, but the last girl she'd taken had an especially large pool, filling a whole blade on her own. She checked each blade with satisfaction before returning to her chair. The rest of the night passed in dark silence with a dying candle and Kas' shuffling feet moving from room to room, sometimes muttering nonsense to himself.

The smell of the factories always disgusted Lillith, no matter what body she inhabited her nose still wrinkled at the smell of coal, flame, heat and sweat, making her uncomfortable in ways she still didn't fathom. She walked down the street, her nostrils wrinkling at the strange fumes that seemed to permeate the air, her head swivelling back and forth as she search for the nearest factory. The brown, dirty dress Lillith wore allowed her to fit perfectly into her surroundings.

On this road every sight was identical, offering some different misty factory with the same miserable workers. Every grey brick on the cobbled street was identical, something Lillith would find deeply satisfying if only it didn't make her feel so nauseous. Those who walked the streets around her all shared the same look, that of a person stumbling towards an executioner's block and Lillith did her best to copy those looks as she weaved in and out of groups. It seemed those walking to work that day were ignorant of the fact that they worked in luxury compared to any demon unlucky enough to be put to work in a factory.

As though agreeing with her, Lillith heard a series of small, weak cries to her left causing her head to snap sharply around to the left in search of its source.

But instead of children she was greeted with a strange new sight; an open factory with no doors or gates, letting dust and smoke billow into the streets rather than keep it inside to leave through chimneys. A small, ragged roof stood overhead, offering little to no shelter to the workers and offering no protection from the rain for the fires of the nearby forge. Underneath this shell of a roof, set around the forge performing different tasks and motions were demons; not the human Newar but, rather, with only brown worn rags to hide their genitalia, their true forms. From head to toe their charcoal skin was cracked all over. Usually, for a healthy demon, these cracks would be the colour of a raging fire, a mixture of orange and blue that flowed beneath their skin, but for these demons they were grey, used coals with the occasional flicker or spark of ember. Their usually bright red hair was browned by dust and dirt that had set in after days, weeks, months or years of endless labour with no respite. Their ribs, thin shoulders and tiny wrists were on display to show off their malnutrition like a trophy they could be proud of, or a brand that was embarrassing to look at directly. Their scars, on the other hand, emblazoned in white were a sign of ownership like nothing else and were always found disturbing the black on their backs. Lillith stopped to watch them for a moment and, as though sensing her presence, their heads cocked and they all slowly turned toward her, like a feral pack driven by the sight of prey. They saw straight through the girl's disguise, but remained silent despite this, staring in confusion, fear or possibly both. Lillith started to panic as people lining the streets noticed the stares and joined the demons in the strange act. The world froze as the girl realised she would be suspected, then questioned, any second now. But if she walked then she would be stared at even more for her ignorance. All she could do was stand still and accept the stares of her brethren, the thing that would be her downfall.

Then, there was a shout of anger and people started walking making the demons drop their stares immediately and go back to work as though nothing had happened as the back door of the factory opened. The man that emerged from it was easily as large as Gairn. He wore a leather jerkin over a tight sweater that did little to hide his bulky arms and chest. His stomach protruded out slightly, which only added to his size. He reached to the belt of his jerkin and pulled out a whip that broke out into six metal tipped ends. The girl turned and quickly walked away as the sounds of metallic whips and demonic screams reached her ears. Lillith had never felt more grateful to be one of the Newar as she fought every impulse in her body that told her to go back and protect her people.

She continued to walk.

As she moved deeper into the industrial zone of the town the air felt heavier and thicker around her, assaulting her nostrils and mouth until she could feel herself almost gagging on the smoke and fumes. She hated new bodies because their senses were always overwhelmed by anything even remotely uncomfortable. The image of the demons in the factory flashed back to Lillith and she immediately remembered just how lucky she was to not be among them. Biting her lip at the thought, she put her head back down and kept trudging forward. A large, dark construct appearing off in the distance. Smoke blooming out of its many chimneys to darken the skies.

The girl had kept one skill from all her previous bodies and that was the ability to blend into a crowd and glide through it as though not there. So Lillith put her head down, no smile, no grimaces, just a neutral face of a busy child moving amongst the dark-clothed and dark natured men and women before they'd even realised she was there. A crowd of humans was the safest place that a Newar could be in, for a time.

Before long, Lillith started to notice more and more children joining the street crowds, all dressed shabbily with dirty faces and dirtier hair, some with various spots of infection and illness blemishing their young faces. She stopped studying their forms immediately, checking herself as she did so. The closer she looked, the more human and childlike her targets became. It was only natural really any closer studying of these sorry emaciated figures and their features made them more real to Lillith. It was easier to see them as nothing more than meals for survival or weapons in the battle against any that threaten her survival. It was the only way for her to continue this grim business.

The girl smiled and she knew she was getting close to the factory where she could work on getting hold of a new body for Gairn she knew he always preferred larger boys as, for some reason, their bodies lasted a little longer for him than a fragile girl's. Lillith took care to hide her smile and not allow anything to distinguish her from the other children. She knew where she was going, she just had to be patient now.

That's when she felt the eyes and their waves. Eyes as black as night invaded her every thought before reaching her vision and seeing through her. She forced the small amount of magic she had to push these eyes away and banish them from her head, but within seconds they returned with even more force than before, flooding her mind with even more force. The girl couldn't even react to the overwhelming assault before she felt herself taken by it and drowned out by the ever-growing eyes.

Every demon horror story would involve these creatures, Reapers. They seemed to be the only creatures that could make a demon fear and despise humanity more than they already did. Whether it was as a symbol of death, the ever-relentless villain, or a simple omen of dark times ahead, Reapers represented this to the demons above any other sign or symbol. They were beings that could only be described as 'darkness'.

Lillith knew if she didn't escape those eyes then she would be driven mad by their empty knowing gaze, a gaze that took only a moment to empty her mind of all sense and reason. They already began to pick at her senses. The misty streets began to blur, and Lillith had to fight hard to not fall over. She kept going in a straight line, remaining in groups of people which were now beginning to form into clumps of brown rags and light skin. As she walked, the hazy images shrank to her height and she couldn't work out if she was among children or the eyes had started to feed her hallucinations. Lillith fought back against the magic as they continued to burn into her senses as though searching for something. She used her magic to push the eyes away and, with resistance, they inched back far enough from her mind to sharpen Lillith's vision and let her compose herself. She pushed the eyes again, this time putting ground between herself and this dark invasion, enough ground for her to take back a small amount of control and brace herself for another assault.

Then, the spell just disappeared entirely and left Lillith alone in her own head, as though the eyes had grown bored and given up. She looked up to find herself in a line of other children leading to a large doorway elevated on a wooden stage. Finally, she sighed with relief, she'd reached the factory where she could find a new child for Gairn. A set of wooden gates slammed shut behind her, the girl realised she must have stepped through them while fighting off the Reaper's eyes.

Smile fading away to nothing, Lillith soon realised something was not right as the line of children heading up to the factory were stuck in a terror-filled silence. Their jovial and chatty nature was overcome by an eerie silence. It shook the girl slightly and made her nervous, so she looked up, going onto her tiptoes to see the large wooden stage more clearly. What she saw made her chest tighten and her blood freeze.

The Reaper.

She observed from afar as it checked every child before they entered the factory as she watched these observations Lillith realised every demon's description of a Reaper was accurate. It was a writhing shadow, moving with silence and grace from place to place, gliding elegantly in the same way as a dancer. From its long, straight black hair to its boots, the Reaper was clad fully in clothes as black as night, but its mask was the most striking feature. It seemed to writhe and move with a life of its own, sometimes growing and sometimes clumsily leaving a tendrilled darkness to slip away and be taken away by the wind, the same way ash will blow from a flame. It was featureless, with no holes or gaps for the Reaper to see or breathe through, it served the sole purpose of acting as a sign of the Reaper's authority. It was a status that allowed the Reapers to hunt whoever they wish; answerable only to the king and king's guard. The Newar were the newest threat that the Reapers had set out to eliminate.

They were feared by all, and rightly so.

Lillith's heart began to race when she saw the Reaper wasn't allowing any child to go through without a search. First, it lifted each child's head and stared into their eyes while pressing its other hand against their chest and keeping it there, as though divining their humanity from heart and eye.

The search looked ridiculous, and yet, Lillith knew that the Reaper saw the humanity in the children from these small things, it would only be a matter of time before she was pulled up to the stage and be at the Reapers mercy.

She felt tears rise to her eyes as the line moved ever closer, power radiated around the Reaper, making waves of terror wash over the bodies of any who got too close, the coldness of this power, even from such a distance, chilled Lillith, giving her goose-bumps under her dress. She kept staring at the Reaper with morbid curiosity as though she was trying to understand him. He checked another child and roughly pushed him through the entrance of the factory before standing again and looking up.

The Reaper looked straight at Lillith and she felt chills assault her anew as they made eye contact and she didn't need to see his face to know the Reaper was smiling, she set off, running without even knowing what she was doing. She had to get back to the inn, get back to Gairn and leave this city before the Reaper found her.

The girl didn't care who saw her or what passersby thought as she just mindlessly ran. The gates were quickly pulled open by a nervous guard, so Lillith dashed through them and out into the streets. The Reaper just stared after the fleeing girl and she knew, deep down, he was laughing.

~*~

"What do you mean we have to leave?" Gairn said, his eyes drawn with worry. There was ash dotting everywhere he stepped on the ground, showing the next stage of his body breaking down. In only a matter of days it would break off of Gairn like a skin and leave him exposed as a demon.

While still large and strong, Gairn's body also began to look older. His hair was greying and falling out in places and, if human, he would have most likely been consigned to a wheelchair at this point. Deep decay seemed to have overcome his skin and it began to flake in places while a slight smell of rot seemed to follow him around incessantly. Lillith ignored this weakened state and his arguments and continued packing. He sighed dismissively and made a motion to argue with his arms but she took no notice as Gairn sat back down, breathing deeply as though this small argument exhausted his continually weakening body.

"I'm just saying, couldn't you be overreacting a little bit? Sure, there was a Reaper there and you did well to escape and you know how those things are. They'll appear as omens and then disappear again as though they were never there to begin with. Maybe he didn't notice, or he lost interest because if he wanted you dead then he would have killed you already if you're convinced he's so terrifying. Either way, you shouldn't worry. We should stay holed up here and keep trying to get me a new body."

"You weren't there!" The girl slammed her fist against the wall in fury, making Gairn flinch back a little. "You didn't *feel* him, he crawled into my mind like it was an open door and played with me, it didn't even seem like he was trying to catch me. All the stories are true, there's nowhere we can hide from him and nowhere we can run."

Gairn lifted his arms in the air to protest again before letting them fall to his side in exasperation. "Okay, so what do you suggest?"

"I suggest that we pack up and leave tonight, leave the city unseen and maybe we can get to another town in a couple of days before your body completely breaks down and we can work on staying undercover again and start fresh." Lillith, without another word, turned and started wrapping up her clothes. Gairn stood there in shock for a moment before slowly walking over to her and placing his hand on her shoulder tenderly. She slowed down at the touch as Gairn slowly formed his words.

"Hey, why don't you sit down and calm down for a second as you've had a tough day. Kas isn't here at the moment so I'll get one of the maids from downstairs to get you a drink…"

Lillith shoved Gairn away, "We are leaving! I am not letting it catch me. You don't understand of course you don't understand. This is more important than your new body, more important than this inn and more important than anyone in this town. Reapers kill Newar, so don't bother denying it. He isn't going to give up and when he finds me he won't just kill me, he'll drive me mad and destroy me completely. I can't let that happen!"

As Lillith screamed the door to her wardrobe burst open and a gust of wind emerged that made her blades rattle and clatter together sending out warped shreds of red magic. The candle burned brighter on her work table and flames flickered angrily around the room as though even the shadows ran to hide from the child's outburst. For a short moment, as she screamed, Lillith felt powerful. Gairn, the light, the shadows and the air herself cleared a space for her. *This is how the Reaper must feel every second,* she mused before the power left her drained and empty.

She stumbled and fell to her knees as the swords stopped swinging and the light of the candle died down to a weak flame. She looked at the floor and watched a single tear fall to the wooden panels and it was soon followed by a flood of them, heavy sobs wracked her body and the girl was powerless to stop them. After a moment's hesitation, Gairn walked over and lifted Lillith tenderly to her feet and gripped her shoulders as he looked into her eyes with obvious concern.

"Okay, we can leave, but if we leave tonight and the town guards catch us acting like stowaways then that'll raise suspicion. Think rationally. If you want to leave then we can wait till morning where we can use some of our leftover gold to get on a carriage so we'll be in a crowd, we'll stay quiet and won't make conversation with anyone there. This way, we'll get to a town a lot faster so hopefully my body won't break down on the trip and we'll find a new one to keep me going as soon as possible." Lillith looked at Gairn before giving a small smile to him through her sobs. She broke away and sat on the bed with her head in her hands.

"Fine, you have a point. We'll rest tonight and then first thing in the morning we'll leave this town behind." She continued to smile at him. "I liked it here, you know. The neighbours were naïve and the staff was nice. But the longer we stay here the more and more we put ourselves at risk. You know that, right?"

"Yes, I understand. We've stuck together for years and you've managed to keep us alive so, if you think we aren't safe here then I'll follow you wherever you want to go. I trust you." Gairn tried smiling but ended up giving the same hungry, toothed look that he always did. Lillith smiled in appreciation of his attempt, looking far more convincing.

Tomorrow, they would leave the town and put as much distance between themselves and the Reaper as they could.

Lillith's smile dropped at the sound of a knock on a door and the small voice of icy cold death. It was the chuckling voice of the Reaper.

The night, still, silent and unmoving was illuminated by the sky above. Without a cloud in sight the moon set out casting its ethereal glow on the world below with reckless abandon, leaving the rough and grey-bricked roads paved in a silver glow. The lampposts were like glistening white pillars, filled from root to stem with the white light of magic to illuminate the road for any traveller when the moon's glow wasn't available to do so.

The night left the town empty and devoid of life, the perfect setting for both romantic strolls and business that required the cover of darkness for its transactions.

Empty except for one.

A passer-by wouldn't see him in the cover of darkness, the uniform allowed him to blend into the night despite the writhing black surrounding it. The shadow stood staring at the inn on the opposite side of the street, only holding his interest in one room, one that was still candle-lit and, until moments ago was shaking with tense argument and screams of magic. Even though he allowed the gate to be opened, encouraged the nervous guard to do so and made no attempt to follow the mouse, they still insisted on being hunted down. It made the Reaper sigh; beating the Newar had become too easy, there was no thrill in the hunt anymore.

The Reaper pulled off its mask; the shadows held onto his face for a moment before reluctantly letting go and fading into the air. The Reaper's long black hair shortened and took on a dirty-brown colour. He shed the black uniform as it followed the mask through the wind in shadowy wisps and his clothes underneath were simple, dirty and worn brown cleaners garments. His pale skin shone with sweat while putting on its picture of naïve innocent stupidity. Finally, the Reaper retrieved his broom from where he'd stowed it in the alley and, before entering the inn, Kas put on his best blank smile and headed straight for the stairs, ignored by the cooks and landlady.

His legs shook and trembled slightly, but he was smiling nonetheless as he stopped at the top and went through the door that creaked slightly when he pushed it. Kas looked down the hall and, when he was convinced no one was watching, shadows from the walls, ground and roof fell onto him, clinging to his skin and turning him into the Reaper again in a quick, graceful moment. His hand relaxed on the hilt of his blade as he headed to the door that still had weak candlelight playing beneath it, he quietly knocked on the door and smiled. "Cleaners."

About the Author

River Daniel has been reporting on the suspicious, destructive activities of the body snatchers known as Newar for the last 10 years in the 'Thornden Press', bringing to light the evil of these creatures, only held at bay by Thornden's beloved Reapers.

Away from writing and reporting the truths of Thornden he regularly spends time with his wife and 2 children and preparing to campaign to become a member of the Trivirate chair in order to better the lives of citizens everywhere, ensure the demonic threat is stable and end the Newar for all time.

The Beginning: Edge of War
By R.Malak

February 23rd 2051, Alaska. Time - 6:00 am

Video Recording A smartly-dressed woman wearing a light grey business dress with dark brown eyes and raven black hair appears on screen, her perfect white teeth framed against her light tan skin. *"This is investigative reporter Danielle Evans reporting for BBC News. I've been sent here to Canada with a team of scientists and reporters to investigate the anomalies caused by the appearance of what is now being called Luna 2, or Moon 2.*

"We will be traveling with the 89th United Expeditionary Force under the command of Captain Raymond to investigate these disturbances and report our findings from Eielson Air Force Base."

The camera pans around to show dozens of soldiers in full military battle armor, marching onto a Bell Boeing V-22 Osprey carrying an assortment of hi-tech weaponry.

February 24th 2051, Time - 3:00 pm

Video Recording The reporter appears on screen again, this time in a darkened hangar bay. *"We've just landed at Eielson Air Force Base, which for some reason looks to be deserted with not a single military personnel in sight. I've spoken with Captain Raymond and he has assured me that this is not in the least bit unusual, as all nonessential personnel have probably been evacuated until the situation here has been resolved. Until then he has ordered that we keep the noise level to a minimum and to follow wherever he goes."*

Time – 5:30 pm

Video Recording The reporter's eyes nervously dart left and right as she whispers in a hushed voice, *"We still haven't seen anyone here at the airport, so Captain Raymond has sent a few men out to take a look around the hangar bay, but they still haven't--"*Echoes of gunfire break the silence.*

"--Contact! Contact! Enemy hostiles inbound!"*

The camera swings side to side as the cameraman and soldiers begin running, followed by a loud, deafening roar that reverberates through the air.

Time- 9:15 pm

Video Recording The young journalist, covered in sweat stains, stares off into the distance, her mouth working up and down trying to speak, while ahead of her a handful of soldiers take up defensive positions around the hangar bay door. The grim silence only broken by the wounded crying out for help and the occasional crackle of gunfire that rattles off from inside the military airbase until at last she finally speaks, her voice quiet and quavering, *"...If you're watching this recording, please listen to me. Captain Raymond's team has been attacked by strange creatures in black armor. They appeared out of nowhere...all around us and just...blood everywhere...We managed to escape back to the hangar bay, but the plane isn't working. Something tore through one of the turbines. We've sent out distress calls, but no one has replied. Please, if you get this message, send help!"*

In the distance, high in the sky, a black dot appears, rapidly growing larger and larger in size. The soldiers, reacting swiftly to the new threat, fire their weapons before turning tail and backing away, a fireball hurtles towards them...then nothing.

~ * ~

Location: *Great Falls, Montana. Year 2051*

Samuel, having only recently returned home from his tour of duty out of Europe, had decided to spend the next few days relaxing with his family, lounging on a worn out couch well past its prime and drinking bourbon while watching the Philadelphia Eagles play the New York Jets. Both teams' performances were fairly underwhelming, but it helped keep his mind off of his friends still serving overseas.

"Daddy! Daddy!" Hearing his little girl call out for him, Samuel quickly stood up, switched off the plasma screen and headed down the hallway towards his daughter's bedroom, where he found Annabel sitting up in bed, tears in her hazel brown eyes, shivering uncontrollably, her curly dark hair a complete mess.

Smiling gently, he walked over to her bedside and sat down beside her, wrapping an arm around her incredibly thin shoulders. "What's wrong, my little princess?"

She pressed her face into his chest and mumbled, "Monsters were chasing me and I couldn't find you. Promise, promise, you won't leave me again."

Samuel brushed his calloused fingers through her hair, and bent down to kiss her on the top of her head. "I'm sorry, sweetie, but I can't make you that promise."

She looked up at him with tear-stained cheeks and asked, "Why? Why can't you stay with me?"

Samuel felt his heart ache at her softly spoken words, his mind conjuring up images of his friends laughing and playfully joking with each other, telling each other stories to help lift their spirits while gunfire echoed off in the distance.

He looked down into her watery brown eyes and wiped her tears away with his sleeve. "It's daddy's job, honey, so I might have to leave sometimes but know this. No matter what happens, I will always come back to you and one day in the future, I'll never leave. I promise. Now get some sleep, sweetie, we have a big day tomorrow."

It took a few seconds for Annabel to remember the plans they'd laid out for the next day before her face scrunched up in excitement, grinning and lying back down in the bed.

Samuel tucked the bed sheets in around her tiny frame and kissed her forehead. Annabel crinkling up her nose as his beard brushed against her cheek. He stood up to leave, glancing back over his shoulder to see if she was still awake and smiled as he saw that she had already nodded back off to sleep. The teddy bear she had so fondly named Squishy Pants was lying on the bedroom floor beside her, a sad reminder of how fast she was growing up and how little time he had gotten to spend with her.

He slowly closed the door behind him so as to not wake her and walked towards his bedroom to get some sleep. Tomorrow would be a big day for them both. He would be meeting up with Miranda to hopefully discuss the idea of him spending a little more time with Annabel, a discussion he was not exactly looking forward to.

~ * ~

Used to waking up early in the morning, Samuel rolled out of bed at 4:00 am, made up his bed and went down the hall to the bathroom to brush his teeth. Butterflies fluttered through his stomach as he pictured seeing Miranda again.

They had split up almost two years ago when she had given up all hope that he would ever quit the army, claiming that he loved the military more than he loved them. It was a sad but familiar tale for many young men and women who had spent their entire lives serving in the armed forces. He'd tried explaining to her why he had to keep going back, but she could never really understand. There were just some bonds that could not and should not be broken.

In the end, though, Samuel didn't really blame her for leaving him. She had taken care of Annabel for years without a single complaint, but years apart had strained their relationship to the point they felt like they were complete strangers. All those wonderful memories they had shared together had been pushed back to the furthest recesses of their minds to scab over, before being ripped back open again each time he saw her.

Simply being near her…seeing her again…was usually enough to bring up memories from the past and make him wonder if he should have tried harder to keep her in his life. But that thought always circled back to the reason they had separated in the first place. Turning his back on the army had never really been an option for him. He'd spent most of his childhood and adult life moving from one army base to the next. It made him feel like he had an extended family, one he had known for many years.

Shaking his head, Samuel picked up the toothbrush and went back to work brushing his teeth, spat, rinsed out his mouth with water before going to check on Annabel when he heard the phone ring.

Skin prickling with a sudden sense of dread, Samuel left the bathroom and slowly walked back towards the kitchen door. The phone still braying loudly as he thrust open the door. His eyes immediately went to the red blinking light at the other end of the room, where the XV series intercom was attached to the wall, displaying the words "private number" across the small screen in bold, black letters. Moving across the room, he stretched out his hand to tap the screen.

"Hello."

"Samuel, listen we have a--" The phone line cut out to be replaced with a message.

"This is an emergency broadcast from the United States Government. For your own safety, all civilians living in Washington, Montana, North Dakota, and Minnesota must immediately evacuate. This is for your own safety. This message will repeat.

This is an emergency broadcast from the United States Government. For your own safety, all civilians living in Washington, Montana, North Dakota, and Minnesota must immediately evacuate. This is for your own safety. This message will repeat..."

Stunned, he stood there listening to the message yet again when the television switched on by itself, a warning siren began to ring, and the same message from the phone appeared on screen with a robotic voice repeating the message.

Quick-stepping it into the lounge room, Samuel picked up the remote and switched it to the news channel where a clearly frightened news reporter stood in front of a busy intersection packed full of cars, their horns blaring repeatedly with mobs of people rioting in the streets behind her, smashing glass windows and burning cars.

His mind raced with possibilities from a terrorist attack to a full-blown invasion, but neither seemed really possible to him. It just didn't make any sense. He collected his thoughts, thinking on his next move when the earth shook beneath him and a roar full of primal rage blasted through the air, sending shivers down his spine.

Trembling a little, he looked out the window to search the street below him for the source of the roar and saw fire raining down from above, engulfing houses and causing cars to explode in a thunderous blast of heat that spread the flames.

"DADDY!"

Jerked back by the sound of his daughter's panicked voice crying out for him, Samuel sprinted towards the bookshelf where he kept his Beretta M9 hidden, fed the magazine into the slot and raced down the corridor.

Cocking the weapon as he ran, he flung open the door to Annabel's room and was confronted by the sight of a massive gaping hole in the side of her bedroom wall. Through it he saw an immense shadowy form high above, winging its way across the clouds. Annabel was curled up into a tight little ball in the corner of the room and was crying into her arm, whimpering with each thunderous explosion that rocked the ground, rocking herself back and forth.

Heart in his throat at the thought of her being injured, he crossed the room in two strides and bent down in front of her, checking her for any cuts or wounds from the explosion that had torn through the building. He gave an inward sigh of relief upon seeing that she was completely unharmed.

Picking her up in his arms, he hugged her to his chest. "It's okay, honey. Daddy, won't let --" Annabel let out a high piercing shriek, which deafened his ears.

He whipped his head around to see why she had screamed. Scrawny green-skinned creatures in brown robes clambered in through the gaping hole in the wall. Their long, pointed ears twitched. Drool dripped from mouths filled with razor-sharp teeth and hungry, yellow eyes stared at them with a savage desire.

Military training kicked into gear. He raised his Beretta and fired, knocking back one of the green-skinned creatures with a shot to the chest and retreated back towards the corridor with his daughter crying in his arms. The creatures, startled at first by the gunfire, became agitated by the death of one of their kin and sent spears flying through the air towards him, forcing Samuel to backpedal quickly and spin on his heels. Jagged spearheads punching into the walls and door behind him.

Filled with a rush of adrenaline and fear for his daughter's safety, he tore through the corridor, looking back over his shoulder in case the creatures were following him and raced out into the street barefoot where he was met with scenes of utter mayhem. People bleeding from wounds ran through the streets, chased by huge green-skinned monsters while fireballs careened overhead to destroy homes and burn people alive. The thick stench of death and smoke permeated the air, and the braying of sirens deafened the ears.

Jonathan, his long-time friend and next door neighbour, burst out of his home looking utterly dazed, a spear embedded deep in his chest, clutching the bloody stump where his left hand used to be. Blood spurted into the air with each step he took before he collapsed in a pool of his own blood. Seconds later the same creature he'd seen in his home erupted out of the doorway behind Jonathon to sink its teeth into his neck and tear out a chunk of his flesh into its bloody maw.

Heart pumping, with no time to think on the nightmarish events unfolding around him, Samuel hurried over to the side of the Rhino GX, a vehicle made to appear much like a military Humvee, pressed his thumb to the key lock and jumped inside, slamming the car door shut just as more spears flew toward him, chipping away at the black paint.

Popping his daughter down in the seat beside him, he tapped the ignition on and felt the engine rumble to life. He quickly switched gears and stamped his foot down on the gas pedal.

He swung the car out of the driveway and sped into the street, dodging and weaving around burnt-out wreckages on the road, and made a swift right turn into a quiet side street. There, he slowed down to a halt and turned to Annabel who was shaking uncontrollably, her shoulders moving up and down. He tried to think of something to say to her but for some reason the right words would not come to him.

He brushed the hair out of her eyes and leaned over to strap her in, whispering a prayer to keep them both safe before starting back up again. Suddenly he was confronted by the image of his ex-wife alone, surrounded by those creatures.

Palms sweating and mouth dry with fear, Samuel increased his speed and made another right turn to head in the direction of Black Eagle and tapped on the dashboard screen to activate voice commands. "Call Miranda." An animation of a phone ringing shook on the screen with no answer.

Terrified something might have happened to her, he accelerated even faster. "Call Miranda!" The phone began ringing again before Miranda appeared on screen without makeup, her long brown hair in complete disarray, her face pinched with worry.

"Samuel, is that you! What the hell is going on?! Is Annabel okay?! Please tell me she's okay!"

"Calm down, Mira, Annabel is fine. Where are you right now?"

"Oh, thank goodness! Annabel, sweetie, can you hear me? It's mommy. Are you okay?"

Samuel repositioned the dashboard screen, so Miranda could see her daughter in the passenger seat beside him.

Releasing an audible sigh of relief at the sight of her, Miranda continued, "It's going to be okay, sweetie. Everything is going to be okay. Daddy is going to keep you safe and bring you home to me. So you have to listen to whatever he tells you to do. Will you do that for me, sweetie?"

Annabel nodded her head up and down, filling him with pride.

Miranda smiled warmly. "That's my tough little cookie. I'll see you both soon. Sam, I'm sending you the address. Please, hurry."

He nodded his head. "Stay safe, Miranda, and don't go outside. I'll be over there as soon as I can." With that final word, he disconnected the call and decided to call Fort Harrison to get some news.

"Call Durkins." The phone rang for a few seconds before it was answered by a tired soldier in full military uniform with short black hair and a hook-shaped nose. After blearily blinking repeatedly, his eyes widened in surprise. "Samuel, is that you! We thought we'd lost you. Thompson has been trying to get into contact with you for hours now. Are you hurt?"

Smiling slightly at his friend's lack of military protocol, he shook his head. "I'm fine, Durkins, although I would like an explanation of what the hell is going on?"

Durkins rubbed a hand across the back of his neck. "I wish I knew, Sam, I wish I knew. All I know is that Alaska went dark a couple of hours after the appearance of Luna 2. Then, next thing we knew, we had reports all along the US-Canadian border of creatures attacking towns and cities. Whatever these things are, it looks like they have taken Canada."

Samuel was stunned tried to think of another question to ask his friend when abruptly the phone line went dead. The dashboard screen darkened and the words "connection lost" popped up. Tapping the screen, he tried to switch it back on, but without success.

Grunting in annoyance, Samuel turned his attention back towards the road and had to swerve aside as an old man materialized right in front of him. Dazed and bleeding from a wicked headwound, the old man wandered through the streets carrying a shotgun, tears flowing freely from his tired red eyes.

Familiar with such pain and loss, Sam bowed his head and kept driving, entering another side street.

More people appeared ahead of him, trying to salvage what was left of their burning homes, still unaware of the monsters that were stalking the streets. The sky was blackened by swirling smoke that seemed to writhe in the air.

Forced to slow down because of all the debris on the road, Samuel found himself almost face to face with a woman in a badly-singed nightgown, hammering at his window. "Please! You've got to help me! My baby is inside! Please! Please! I'm begging you! Save my baby!"

Heart clenching in his chest at the sound of her voice, he shook his head slightly to stop himself from getting out of vehicle and swung the car around her to keep going.

"Fuck you! Fuck you, heartless bastard! Fuck youuuuuu!" she shrieked, wildly punching and kicking the side door.

Annabel, terrified by the desperate woman, began crying softly again.

"It's okay, honey. Everything is going to be okay," he said. Whether that was more for his sake or hers, he didn't really know anymore. All he knew was that he couldn't take any risks with her life.

~ * ~

Location: Black Eagle, Montana. Year 2051

Miranda, beside herself with worry, paced up and down her living room, moving in between her twin white sofas that sat opposite each other and across her Persian carpet. The beautiful mosaic of birds flying through the cloud currents plastered on the wall beside her was no longer able to calm her rapidly beating heart and slow her pulse.

She stared up at the classically-styled clock hanging from the wall above her head while distant howls, gunfire, and explosions barely registered upon her distracted mind. Three hours had almost passed since Sam had called her and, no matter how she tried to run things through her mind, she couldn't help but think that something bad had happened to them. *It shouldn't take him this long to get here from his place!* Unable to help herself, she began to work through the worst possible scenarios: Sam getting into a car crash, monsters attacking them on the road, or worse…

She shook her head, trying to rid herself of all her doubts, hoping with all her heart everything was alright, yet fearing the worst.

She pulled out her phone from the pocket of her jeans and tried to call Sam again. But, once again, the phone went straight to voicemail. Frustrated, she tossed the phone onto the coffee table, causing Greg to look up at her with concern.

Seeing the questioning look in his pale blue eyes, she held up her hand. "I'm fine. I just wish I knew where they were."

Greg nodded his head before thumbing back his glasses, standing up, and straightening his business suit. He walked past her towards the glass screen door that looked out over the balcony into town where smoke and burning fires still dotted the skyline. The fireballs that had come crashing down from the heavens had stopped for the moment.

Back turned towards her, Greg spoke softly, "Honey, I think it's time we considered leaving without them."

Deep in her thoughts, she scarcely heard what he'd said until he swung around to face her. "I think it's time we considered leaving, Mira."

Miranda stopped her pacing and looked up at Greg in shock, her heart growing cold inside her chest. "What did you just say?!"

Stiffening his shoulders, Greg met her hot gaze with a look of desperation. "You heard the news reporter, Miranda! We're supposed to be packing our bags and heading towards the nearest school to be evacuated, not waiting here, hoping your ex-husband will come and save us! We can't stay here, Miranda! It's not safe, not anymore!"

A part of her knew that what Greg was saying made sense, that waiting here was risky, especially when Sam should have already reached them by now. But all she could feel was a white hot rage coursing through her veins at the very suggestion that abandoning her family was somehow the right thing to do.

Hazel brown eyes shining with intensity, she replied angrily, "I can't believe what I'm hearing! I will not leave my family behind, Greg! I don't care how long it takes for them to get here! I'm not leaving them! If you want to go, then go!"

Greg swept forward to grab hold of her by both shoulders. "Please, Miranda! See reason! It's been three hours without a single word from them! Even calculating traffic and congestion, it still should only take them one or two hours at the max to get here!"

Miranda thrust aside his hands, ignoring the hurt look in his eyes, and crossed her arms over her chest. "I'm not leaving, Greg."

Greg sighed heavily, his shoulders sagging and whispered, "If we stay here we'll die, Miranda. You've seen what's out there. We can't stay here. We just can't. I can't."

Unmoved by his words, she took a step back, her expression hardening, and pointed towards the door.

Sighing in resignation, Greg moved towards the front door, pausing at the doorway to look back at her. His eyes pleaded with her once more to reconsider, but she could never do what he wanted her to do. Before he closed the door behind him, she heard the faint words. "I love you, Miranda. I always will."

Drained of all her strength, she collapsed to her knees on the rug, hot tears spilling down her cheeks at the pain she felt wash over her, unable to comprehend how quickly her life had been turned upside-down. She stared at the door, half hoping he would come back and take her into his arms and tell her that he would never leave her. She could almost feel his strong arms around her, holding her tight, and pictured his warm smile that was so full of life…

Heart sinking at the realisation he wasn't coming back, she wiped the tears away from her eyes and stood up. There was no point wallowing in her own self-pity. What's done was done, and if Greg couldn't understand how much her family meant to her, then he hadn't really loved her as much as he said he had. With that stinging thought in mind, she resolved to ready herself for when Sam arrived. Moving toward the kitchen, she threw open the cabinets and pulled out any canned items before searching the house for any bottles to fill with water.

Miranda then packed a bag with three sets of clothing for each of them, framed photos of her family, and other items that would be needed on the trip, when abruptly she heard a loud scream emanate from the hallway outside her apartment complex.

Head whipping up at the anguished sound, she had only a second to think before the front door was blasted open and two hulking creatures in black-plated armor burst into the room. Their tusks dripped red with fresh blood and jagged battle axes covered in torn flesh.

~ * ~

Location: Great Falls, Montana. Year 2051

The drive north for the most part was fairly quiet with cars streaming southbound away from the Canadian border to make their way deeper inland. Making quick progress along the highway, Samuel passed row upon row of cars, shouting and honking at each other in their attempt to move through a clogged bottleneck where a truck had overturned. With no law enforcement to control the situation, men and women jumped out of their vehicles to hurl abuse at each other while a few even went so far as to brawl with each other on the streets. Columns of black smoke billowed around them from the flaming wreckage on the road.

Annabel, exhausted from the journey, lay curled up in the back seat, sleeping, jerking awake every so often in a panic, searching for him.

Nearing the bridge out of Great Falls, Samuel twisted his head to check on her when he heard a distinct popping sound. The steering wheel became difficult to control, and the left side of the car began to make a weird screeching sound, forcing him to make a pit stop at the side of the road.

Annabel, shaken awake by the noise, gasped out, "Daddy?"

"Easy, sweetie, it's nothing, just a blown-out tire. You stay here and take care of the car. I won't be long, I promise."

Lip quivering, she nodded her head and gave him a salute, which made him smile fondly at her.

Clambering out of the Rhino, he stuffed the Beretta into the front of his cargo pants within easy reach and knelt down in front of the blown-out tire.

His knee firmly planted on the hard, rough surface of the road and gritting his teeth, he leaned forward and tugged free a jagged piece of metal that had lodged itself in the wheel, letting out the air. With no way to patch up the tire and refill it, Samuel stood back up and went to the back of the black SUV. He grabbed hold of the spare tire attached to the rear, freeing it from its locking mechanism and rolled the cumbersome wheel over to the side of the car. He then tapped the back door handle to open up the door, peered inside, and picked up the jack and tire iron. He then walked to the front of Rhino where the deflated tire was and went to work.

Around ten minutes passed by in the relative quiet with the sun gradually sinking lower in the sky before he was finally able to unscrew the lug nuts and replace the front wheel.

Sweat dripping down his back, he moved to stand back up when he felt the cold, hard barrel of a pistol pressed up against his skull.

Freezing in place, he prayed that Annabel was asleep in the car before whispering softly, "Listen, I don't have much money, but whatever I have you can have it. Just leave me be."

The man replied with a dry, nasty chuckle. "That's a nice-looking car you have there. You wouldn't mind if I took it for a spin, would you?"

Feeling the barrel of the pistol press harder against his skull, Samuel grimaced, trying to think of a way out of this situation but unable to come up with anything; not without first learning more about the man behind him.

Somehow reading his thoughts, the man leaned forward so Samuel could feel his hot breath against his neck and snapped in a dangerous tone, "Now, now, I wouldn't do anything stupid if I were you. Now get up! And open the door!"

Swallowing the bile rising up at the back of his throat, he looked at the car, which appeared like a moving fortress with its square edges and contours. The tinted windows gleamed. He knew he couldn't allow whoever was behind him inside. As long as his daughter was inside, she was safe from harm.

"I'm sorry, but I can't do that," he replied.

Samuel could sense the man contemplating his next move when he felt the side of the pistol strike the back of his head. Rolling with the blow, he whipped the Berretta out of his belt in one practiced move and fired upwards. Two rounds to the chest and one to the head.

The man touched his fingers to his bleeding chest before stumbling backwards, collapsing onto the side of the road, blood dribbling out from his mouth.

Breathing harshly, Samuel hauled himself back up onto his feet, rubbed the cut on his forehead and walked over towards the dying man. Perhaps thirty years old, the man had thick black stubble along his jawline, a crooked nose that had seen one too many fights, coal-black eyes, and slicked-back hair.

He stared down at the man, wondering who he could have been, before leaning down to pick up the 9mm Glock that had fallen out his grip, catching a glimmer of something out from the corner of his eye. Curious to see what it was, he checked the man's coat pockets and swallowed back a gasp of surprise as he pulled out a police badge.

Shocked and appalled by the revelation, Samuel backed away from the dead body and turned towards the car, trying to grasp what he had done and found Annabel, her face drained of all color, staring at the dead man through the car window.

Rushing to block her view of the corpse, he hid the pistols behind his back and unlocked the car door, causing Annabel to scream and recoil away from him in terror.

Raising his arm up to try and calm her down, Samuel inched closer to her, but she shrunk away even further from him, her eyes filled with fear that cut through him like a hot knife, forcing him back a step. 'So this is what my daughter thinks of the real Samuel' he thought sadly. And though every part of him ached to comfort her and find some way to take away her fear, she was right to fear him. He wasn't the same man she thought he was; something he'd hoped she would never learn.

Shoulders sagging beneath the weight of his thoughts, he opened up the glove compartment to store both of the pistols and got back into the SUV, his head bowed with guilt as he started the car back up and drove towards the bridge in the solemn silence hoping and praying that Miranda would know what to do.

The sky darkening, Samuel switched on the headlights as he drove across the narrow bridge, the river below bare of all life, before exiting the highway onto Montana Avenue and stopping in front of a newly built apartment complex that looked out on the river.

Sighing, he switched off the engine and spoke without looking back at his daughter, "I don't know if you remember this, Anna, but when you were a little girl I would read you bedtime stories about good men and evil witches, brave princes and wicked monsters. Well, sweetie, that is what the world is like right now. There are good people and bad people…"

After a few moments Annabel finally replied, "…Was that a bad man?"

Samuel nodded his head. "He was a very bad man, but that doesn't mean I wanted to hurt him." He twisted his head round to face her. "That's why we have to be more careful and watch out for each other. We don't want the bad men to come and get us."

Annabel bit her lips pensively before asking, "Are you one of the good people?"

Samuel let out a small sigh at her innocent question, disliking the idea of lying to her, but at the same time needing her to trust him. After thinking for a moment, he replied, "I try to be. Now come on, let's go see Mommy."

Pulling out his Beretta from the glove compartment, he got out of the car and waited for her to come out, taking her slender hand in his and walking together toward the apartment building. The moon rose high into the sky to light their path as they entered the vacant foyer and made their way toward the elevator across the white marble tiles.

He pressed the button, waiting for a few seconds before he heard a whooshing sound and the elevator ding as it opened up to let them inside.

Picking up Annabel in his arms, he let her push the button for Miranda's floor. The elevator doors gliding smoothly shut as they ascended rapidly before it let out another ding when they arrived at their destination.

Hairs prickling at the back of his neck at the overwhelming silence, he tightened his grip on Annabel's hand and readied his pistol.

Hallway lights flickered on and off, and a cold breeze blew in through shattered glass windows. His footsteps lightly tapping against the red carpet as he walked towards her apartment, his legs taking him through corridors covered in claw marks with smears of blood darkening the walls.

Samuel tried to cover Annabel's eyes so she wouldn't see the blood and opened his mouth to lie but snapped it shut when he saw the knowing look in her eyes as she too recognised the blood stains for what they were, displaying the same keen intelligence that had led him into falling in love with her mother. However, it still did not lessen the blow at the thought of his daughter having to see such gruesome things, forcing her to grow up.

Saddened by that thought, he continued on down the hallway, whispering another prayer under his breath for Miranda and felt his pulse quicken as he neared her apartment.

Heart thumping loudly in his chest, he turned the last corner and felt a metal fist slam into him and grab hold of his heart. The door to Miranda's penthouse lay in tatters, its hinges twisted up in a mangled heap and its frame shattered into a thousand pieces. And for a briefest of seconds Samuel did not know what to do, all his training and experience gone in an instant of panic that blinded him with fear. Even after all these years apart from her, Samuel still needed Miranda to be okay, he needed her to be safe, and he needed her. The mere thought of her gone from this world, left alone to raise Annabel, punched a hole right through him that he couldn't fix.

"Daddy?"

Broken out of his stupor by the sound of her voice, he looked down into Annabel's eyes which so closely resembled Miranda's and somehow conjured up a smile. No, Miranda couldn't be dead. She was one of few women he knew who would keep her cool under pressure. She would survive this, she could survive this.

He knelt down to squeeze Annabel to his chest, hoping she hadn't seen his momentary lapse, before pulling her gently back and brushing her soft curly hair. "Listen, honey, I need you to wait for me right here. If you see anything, shout as loud as you can and come get me. Okay? I need you to be brave. Can you do that for me?"

She nodded her head furtively but still held tightly onto his hand, her small fingers grasping his as though it were a lifeline.

Ears hot and heart pounding like a drum, he detached himself from her grip and gave her another hug, feeling how small she was in his arms and turned away. He had to know.

Samuel stepped over the shattered door and walked inside. "Miranda? Are you here?"

Hearing no reply, he edged his way forward, gun raised in both hands and saw bloody drag marks on the carpet floor leading toward the living room.

Filled with a heavy sense of dread, Samuel followed the trail of blood before collapsing to his knees and releasing a groan of despair. Miranda, her chest torn open, lay splayed out across the carpet, her body torn open from bowel to stern, her mouth gaping open in a silent scream that didn't quite come out.

Sickened to his core, he crumpled up beside her, head shaking from side to side, praying this was all a figment of his imagination when he caught sight of her hand, lying a few feet from him. The wedding ring he had bought for her years ago, still on her finger, and even after all these years she still wore it; his mother's wedding ring.

He stared at the ring for what felt like an eternity, the pit of his chest empty and eyes full of unshed tears that just wouldn't come. He felt so lost and alone, and yet he couldn't let it all end here. Annabel was waiting for him, and no matter how he felt right now, he couldn't abandon her to this world.

Standing back up as though still in a dream, he headed towards the bedroom and returned with a blanket to cover her.

Samuel gazed one last time into those eyes he had spent so many years staring into, falling in love with, remembering fondly how he had wanted so desperately to spend the rest of his life with her, and kissed her forehead in farewell.

A part of him was dead and gone, but there was still one piece of her that still remained. "I'll keep her safe, Miranda. I swear it. I'll keep her safe," he whispered before getting up, looking back one last time, and heading for the doorway. *I love you, Miranda, and always will...*

Thank you for reading The Beginning: Edge of War.
Book 1 The Beginning: Breath of War
is now available on Amazon.

About the Author

Born in a faraway land, Silverhand has traveled many universes and received his education at the College of Mages. Having dabbled in many forbidden magics his primary obsession still remains the sole conquest of all worlds.

An alchemy enthusiast and an hunter of men, he has pursued various quests and built himself quite the reputation. He has also grown up hearing stories of the fabled Robert Soulstealer, David Deathbringer, Salvatore the Mad, and Wild William.

Robert the Soulstealer is by far and away his greatest inspiration and guiding light.

The Bone Witch
by H.M.R Leeper

"The Witch's heart of ice and stone
Her body bleached as bone.
With drop of blood or strand of hair
Your flesh becomes her throne.

Always flee the pale knight.
Her vicious, cunning might.
Challenge not death's cruel warden,
Or vanish from the light."

An old man hummed the tune to himself. It had been many decades since the Shadow Wars that scoured the western country Orsenia had ended, and peace settled between Witches and Non-Witches. Yet, he still remembered the old folk tales parents used to tell to keep children in at night, when the fighting was at its worst. Tales of a Witch, more demon than human, who puppeted an onslaught of long-dead soldiers against those who stood in her path. Somewhat exaggerated yes, but the old man knew the truth behind the myths. He sat at a large, wooden desk, carefully signing off pieces of paper, the bright glow of newly discovered electricity lighting up the room. In the corner an assistant waited, ready to gather the letters for delivery. Beside her stood a young boy, still new to the job, nervously adjusting the sharp lines of his uniform.

"I'm glad she's gone, Mr Brackett... Folk say she was evil," the boy piped up, making the old man lower his pen to look up thoughtfully. The boy stepped forward as the man gestured for him to approach, ignoring the disapproving shake of the older assistant's head.

"Life is made up of moments, young man. Rearrange the snapshots and you can change a saint into a monster. The way the war painted her, she was evil, a demon. But I knew her differently." Ignoring the grimace of his assistant who had heard this story one too many times, Mr. Brackett smiled gently. "I suppose age gives me more time to look back on those moments... But to me, she was just a girl with no other choice, and I was just an ignorant boy tied to her for better or worse..."

~*~

The first time Jamie Brackett met the Bone Witch was on a chill, grey evening. Jamie had been with his older brother and father at the large outdoor market set up in one of the city's main squares, selling hand-crafted furniture and engraved chests. It had been a long day, and Jamie, being only eight, had grown bored. The temperature dropped as night drew near, and he wished desperately for something exciting to happen. It was little surprise, therefore, that when his family grew distracted with a customer, young Jamie crept away, weaving in between the tightly packed stalls and crowd.

Contrary to the usual type of market, the outdoor market of the city of Newton grew busier as the night progressed. Instead of sunlight, vendors summoned globes of multi-coloured light that bathed the cobbled streets in a comforting glow. Illusionists arrived after their usual work shifts to entertain along the edges of the market, weaving their magic to make strange, glowing beasts burst out of hats, or dancing flames spin stories through the sky. Every now and then the booming sound of an amplified voice calling to customers would echo through the bustling market. Jamie loved to explore here. Now and then he would stop to inspect a stall, peering wide-eyed at the various potions in crystal bottles, or the twinkling talismans hanging amongst the brightly coloured drapes and wooden beams that gave the market some level of shelter.

But soon enough, the young boy found himself completely lost. The realisation of how lost he was dawned on him slowly, like a chill creeping over his body before overcoming it all at once. Jamie fell still, finding himself on the edge of the market. It was darker here, the performers further away and the only lights near him were the pale flickering gas lamps standing haphazardly along the street. It felt as if the shadows were trying to reach out and guide him further into the darkness. From where he stood, he could now hear distant, angry shouts and chants previously masked by the sounds of the market. The voices were too far for him to see their owners, but Jamie knew of the anti-magic protestors. His father had often grumbled about them across the kitchen table to his mother over breakfast.

He didn't move as his breath quickened and his eyes darted in a frantic attempt to recognise where he was. Everything looked different now that darkness had descended. He felt his heart rate double as thoughts of being lost forever raced in his mind. Jamie was as likely to start running in a desperate attempt to find home as he was to simply burst into tears when a small bird landed on the ground just in front of him. The little creature chirped once, staring directly at him, then hopped along the street before turning to look at him again. Whatever, or whoever this bird was, it wanted him to follow. In the mind of an eight year old, the urge to follow such a strange, yet obvious summoning was irresistible.

Without any idea what else to do, and growing colder by the second, Jamie sniffled to himself before slowly following the bird as it hopped and fluttered along the street, chirping encouragement every now and then. It wasn't long before they arrived in front of a small, humble house with a neat wooden porch and a black door. In a creaking rocking chair on the porch sat a young girl, maybe five years older than Jamie. A young tabby cat curled by her feet, and Jamie's little guide flew up to perch on her shoulder. She turned to whisper to the small sparrow, and after a moment it leapt into the air, disappearing swiftly into the night.

The girl turned her attention back onto Jamie.
"You look cold. I have a blanket here." She gestured to the blanket folded on the small table next to her. Jamie hesitated. He so wanted to get warm, but the girl was a stranger, and his father had always warned him to be wary of those he did not know. Jamie didn't have magic like his brother; he had to be more careful.

"Who are you?" She raised an eyebrow, and her thin lips twitched in a smile.

"I'm Hester."

Jamie stared silently. Of all the girls he'd met, he'd never seen one quite like her.

The girl could not have been older than fourteen, with smooth skin paler than any person Jamie had ever met - much lighter than his own. Her equally pale hair fell in a sleek, straight line down her back. It was like all the colour had been leached out of her, apart from the warm brown of her eyes staring impassively at him. Whilst thin, she was in no way skin and bones. It was a wiry type of thin seen in children who spent their days running and playing outside. Hester sat up, tall and straight, and she didn't look away once from his scrutinisation. She was too sharp, like a piece of ice carved to look like a girl. And yet, Jamie didn't feel afraid. He was confused and intrigued, perhaps, but she did not scare him. So he tried to convince himself of that at least.

"I should go... my father's looking for me," he spoke in a soft whisper. Hester smiled again.

"Not to worry. I sent my familiar off to fetch him. Come and sit. I don't bite. Besides, it's dangerous out there alone. Lots of angry people." Her smile wasn't sweet. It was like the baring of teeth. When Jamie didn't move, she sighed, rolled her eyes with a huff and settled back into her chair. "If you want to keep standing there like an idiot, go right ahead. But it's not my fault if you catch a chill." Jamie jumped a little, both at the surprising child-like impatience in her voice and the feeling of the small cat that had woken up and approached to press its soft body against his leg in greeting. Hesitating, he crouched down to scratch behind the ears, smiling when he felt the purrs rumbling through its little figure. When the cat sauntered back to the porch, Jamie followed, quietly sitting cross legged on the floor beside it so he could keep stroking the friendly creature. Neither he nor Hester spoke, although the girl moved once to take the blanket and drape it over his shoulders when he'd started to tremble from the cold.

They sat in silence for what could have been hours or minutes. The only sound to disturb them was the consistent purring of the cat that had found its way into Jamie's lap. When his father found them, announcing the arrival with a shout of joy from Jamie's older brother who had run on ahead, Jamie gently dislodged the cat and stood up. Turning, he froze as his gaze met Hester's. Neither spoke until Jamie bowed his head in a thankful nod.

"It was nice to meet you, Jamie." Hester smiled.

It wasn't until Jamie was safely home with the rest of his family that he paused to wonder how she knew his name.

--- 6 Years Later ---

The second time he visited the Bone Witch's home was on a sunny winter's day. The air was crisp and the sky so blue it hurt to stare too long. In the distance the thick smoke of factories, only a few years old, lining the outskirts of the city wafted high in the air, creating its own dark clouds. Jamie and his brother, Cameron, both now excitable teenagers, had been playing in one of the scrap yards, when Cameron had fallen and pierced his leg on something twisted and sharp. Crying out in pain, he lay on the ground with his leg stretched out as Jamie tied his coat tight around the injury. Cameron's familiar, a small, scruffy fox, whined anxiously, nosing at his side. Through gritted teeth, Cameron spoke.

"I think she lives around here."

"Who, Cam?"

"Hester, y'know, that Witch healer," Jamie hesitated. He knew exactly who Cameron was talking about.

"I dunno, Cam. Ma says she's a necromancer, works with the dead. I'd be scared of her touching me."

Despite his grimace of pain, Cameron couldn't help but let out a short laugh, wincing as he tried to stand.

"Good thing I'm the one that needs healing then. C'mon, she lives just down the road I reckon. In that little house on Remis Street." He tried to put weight on the injured leg, taking a sharp breath, before forcing a few steps. "Besides, none of the hospitals will see me. Won't help Witches no more." Cameron had a point and wouldn't take no for an answer. It was clear from the way he winced and groaned with each step he couldn't walk for long. The house wasn't far from the scrap yard.

Reluctantly Jaime nodded, stooped down to support his brother and limped towards the street. While some people stared openly at the strange sight of the fox and two boys, both dirt-covered and one bleeding down his leg, most chose to ignore them. Or perhaps luck was simply on their side today. No passing stranger stopped to ask questions, none of the carts or horse-drawn carriages spared second glances for them. Ultimately, it didn't take long to find the quaint little house that doubled as Hester's shop and home.

Like the first time he had met her, Hester was on her front porch. She was older now, about 19, and her hair was longer. But beyond that, little had changed. An elderly tabby cat was lounging in a basket near her chair, basking in the warm sunlight. Red paint had been slashed across the front of her home in a crude message. As Jamie approached, he could see where Hester had been working to wash it off.

"Please, can you help us? My brother's hurt." Jamie tentatively asked. His voice came out as a nervous squeak, which drew a sharp blush to his dark cheeks, especially when Cameron let out a quiet snort of amusement. Jamie hadn't spoken to Hester since the night she had watched over him. Hester tilted her head before pushing up the sleeves of her plain cotton dress.

"I can see that. Come inside and get him up on the kitchen table. Do hurry, blood is such a pain to clean off floorboards." With a cursory scowl at the paint still staining her home, she vanished through the black door, leaving it open for the brothers. Jamie didn't hesitate. He could feel Cameron leaning heavily on him as his brother struggled to stay upright. He'd lost a lot of blood, which was clear from the ashen colour of his skin as Jamie half-dragged him into the house.

With some help from Hester, they managed to get Cameron lying on the table.

"I need you to hold him down. Removing the scrap is going to hurt and if he moves it will make the wound worse." She spoke in a stern, no-nonsense tone of someone far older as she pulled on a worn apron, with faded brown stains across the fabric.

"Wait, you're just going to pull it out? What if he bleeds too much? What if you tear something else?" Before he could ask any more, the girl reached over and pressed a finger to his lips.

"No more questions. Unless you want me to waste more time while your brother bleeds out?" A small whimper from Cameron kept Jamie quiet, and he shook his head quickly. Holding down his brother, he nodded to Hester who, after carefully slicing the trouser leg with a wicked looking knife, gripped the scrap of metal. With a hard tug, the metal was pulled free and new blood flooded to the surface. Before Jamie could voice his concern, however, Hester dropped the scrap onto the table and placed both hands over the injury. Her eyes were shut in concentration, and her eyelids fluttered rapidly as her lips mouthed strange words.

Silence stretched between them. Cameron had passed out from the pain and lay deathly still. Jamie could barely see the slow rise and fall of his chest - only if he looked very closely. But Jamie was more focused on Hester's hands. Dark veins stood out from her paper-white skin, and a strange light seemed to pulse between her fingers. The gas-lights flickered like an erratic heartbeat. Hester's face was twisted into a concentrated scowl, and for a moment it seemed as if the entire house held its breath. Then, the lights returned to their steady, rosy glow. Cameron's breathing became rhythmic and deep.

As Hester stepped back from her patient, pausing to wipe away the blood from his skin, Jamie could see a faint puckered mark where the metal had pierced his brother. The skin had sealed together in a neat line. Hester meanwhile, looked tired. Dark bags had blossomed like bruises beneath her eyes, and she leaned against one of the kitchen chairs as she surveyed her work.

"That should do nicely. He'll have a stiffness in his leg for the next week or so, and he should take it easy for the next three days. No running or long-distance walking for two weeks, minimum." She stated firmly, fixing Jamie with a look that allowed no argument. So Jamie nodded his head in understanding, starting to rummage in the depths of his pockets.

Pulling out a few copper and silver coins, he laid them out on the table. Hester raised an eyebrow as she watched, carefully cleaning her hands with a wet cloth.

"How much do I owe you? I don't have much. This is all I have on me now, but if you're willing to wait until the end of the week I can get more. I promise I'll be good for it." Before he could continue his assurances, Hester raised a hand, silencing him.

"You're a lot more talkative than when we last met. Feel free to keep your money."

"But... But you saved his life. You used magic! I can't just take your services for free. It isn't right!" He protested with a stubborn shake of his head. It drew a smile across Hester's lips.

"Very well. In return for my services, you owe me a debt of one favour. I don't know what for, and I can't tell you when. But when I ask, you will say yes. Do you accept this payment?" Jamie took a reluctant step towards her now outstretched hand.

"...I don't have any magic. I'm not much use for someone who has it. Are you sure there isn't something else I can do? Maybe, I can work for free as your assistant until the debt is paid?" But Hester only shook her head.

"I have enough assistants, and they aren't half as chatty as you." A chuckle and nod of her head indicated the two skeletons tucked in the corner that Jamie hadn't noticed. Of course. Why hire an assistant when you could create your own with complete obedience?

"A favour. That's all I ask. Just one. Do we have a deal, Jamie Brackett?" He stared at the pale hand held out to him. There wasn't much else he could offer her, and with the rest of his family unable to find work due to having magic, every penny of his own meagre earnings was desperately needed. With a sigh, Jamie reached out to clasp it in his own dark hand, jolting in surprise at how cold her skin was to the touch.

"We have a deal."

--- 9 Years Later ---

The third time Jamie visited the home of the Bone Witch took some time to occur. Jamie grew from an awkward teenager to a nervous young man. The angry protests and anonymous vandalism of his childhood had grown with him. Over the past year Witches had been slowly disappearing, taken from their homes by armed guard. Unregistered Witches were arrested. Those thought to be practising dangerous magic soon followed. There seemed to be no reason for some of the latest disappearances. Perhaps it was ignorance, or privilege, but Jamie hadn't taken much notice of the disappearances until his own brother was taken.

He had begged as Cameron was dragged out the door, his familiar muzzled and bound in a small crate. Jamie pleaded for an audience with the King, hoping his job in the palace would give him a greater chance of being heard. No answer. Instead, he was forced to continue his duties and go about his day, whilst horrors of what could be happening to Cameron haunted his thoughts.

Now and then Jamie would bump into Hester. Often in the small, secret markets that popped up around the city for an hour or two, then vanished without a trace, only to appear the next week somewhere else. Gone were the days of the lavish marketplace where his father had sold carvings and furniture. It was one of those visits on a crisp early morning, as he carefully followed directions to the next market, that he was stopped.

A small bird had swooped low over his head and landed in front of him. It cocked its head before chirruping loud enough to grab his attention and stop Jamie from stepping on its small form. Jamie stared down at the bird.

"What are you doing out here on your own? You'll be in trouble if you're caught." The bird hopped a little and tweeted back, as if to declare itself unafraid of such a threat. Jamie smiled at the bold little sparrow, and as it hopped a few spaces away, he began to follow.

"Did she send you to find me?" As always, the bird didn't speak, simply chirping as it led the way, taking flight once it was sure Jamie was following.

The familiar flew along back alleys, leading Jamie to arrive at a recognisable, if faded, black-doored house for the third time. Nine years later and Hester still greeted him as she had before. Pale as ever, her hair was cut short now. Both frowns and laughter had left faint creases on her skin. She sat in the comfortable chair on the somewhat run-down porch with a small, black book in her hands. The rattle of bones revealed an animated feline skeleton as it stretched and rolled over on a plush cushion.

"I thought it was illegal to reanimate the dead?" She gave a cursory glance over her shoulder at the skeleton-cat, then back up to Jamie.

"Nikeet causes no harm. Her old bones aren't up to much hunting." Smiling at her own joke and ignoring an actual answer, Hester rose to her feet and beckoned for Jamie to come inside.

He didn't wait for another invitation, instead following her steps and shutting the faded black door behind him. Peering around the room, he got flashes of the last time he had visited.

"You were able to get the blood out then?"

"Hmn? Oh, yes. There wasn't too much, it was mostly on the two of you. Tea?" Jamie nodded, and Hester went to boil water in an iron-wrought kettle over a small fire keeping the house pleasantly warm. Jamie took a seat at the kitchen table, smiling as the sparrow familiar flew to perch on Hester's shoulder, twittering away. He could never fathom how a Witch understood their familiar's speech. It had always sounded like a normal animal's growls and squawks to him. But Hester seemed to nod and murmur responses, before taking the kettle off the fire and pouring two cups of tea. She handed him one then took a seat, both hands clasped around her own cup, cradling it close for warmth. Jamie jumped as he felt something hard rubbing against his leg. A quick look down confirmed it was the skeleton-cat pressing against him as it sauntered past. Each step made the bones rattle and clack softly, held together only by Hester's magic. Jamie watched the cat make its way to its small bed by the fire where it curled up again to do what he supposed was the closest thing a skeleton could get to sleeping.

The house was cosier than the last time he'd entered. The room was clean with the faint smell of baked bread still lingering in the air. Each chair had home-made cushions - simple but comfortable to sit on, and a small painting of two women smiling with their arms around one another stood on the mantelpiece above the cheerfully crackling fire. One of the women in the picture looked a lot like Hester. He smiled at the sight, before his thoughts were interrupted as Hester cleared her throat.

"I was sorry to hear about your brother." The ache in his chest doubled at the mention of Cameron.

"I miss him. I tried to appeal for his release but," He sighed into his cup. "Well, you probably know how it is."

"I do… But that wasn't what I was talking about." Jamie looked up sharply, staring into the dark eyes of the Witch. "You don't know?" She paused, frowning in deliberation. Jamie thought he caught a glimpse of soft sorrow behind the sharpness of her face. "Cameron is dead, Jamie. I'm sorry you're only finding out now, and from me of all people… But he passed about a month ago." Despite the warm crackling of the fire, Jamie felt ice cold. Neither he nor Hester looked away from each other as his brain came to a halt. Dead. All those months he'd tried to fight for Cameron, and he was gone.

"How do you know?" Jamie managed to croak. For a moment he thought he could see sympathy in her expression. It was the expression of someone who had delivered bad news before, who had seen the range of human reactions to it, and knew the pain she was giving.

"Through what *was* my 'official job'. It's why they haven't arrested me yet. They kill prisoners who refuse to plead guilty or answer questions, and brought me in to reanimate them. Made me force the spirit to answer questions. If the prisoner's innocent… Well, they didn't tell me what they did with the information after I got it." Her expression had twisted into a grimace, her knuckles white as her hand shook a moment around the cup she still held.

"You work for those monsters?" Jamie spat out, banging a clenched fist against the table.

"Worked. Past tense. And anyway, don't you? We do what we must to survive, Jamie. I worked for them so I wouldn't end up like countless others; like half of my neighbours and all of my friends, like the woman I loved. You can't honestly tell me you haven't noticed the number of Witches dwindling to nothing over the last few years? The way we've been blacklist from vital public services? Or the way the weakest of us got run out of town by god damned mobs? Being a Witch is a death sentence, and if agreeing to help with distasteful work kept me alive, what choice did I have?" She didn't flinch at his burning rage, matching it with a fierce glare of her own. Unlike Jamie, Hester didn't slam her hand down or shout. Her voice was low and steady and held the threat of a woman with no choices left to make.

Silence spread between them, until Jamie drew abruptly to his feet.

"If that's all you wanted, then I should be going." He was cut off by her cold hand wrapped around his wrist. Hester's stare was intense, and without arguing, he sat down again.

"I know you're in shock. I know you want to grieve and rage and process. And I know you probably want to hate me. I'm sorry, but don't have time for that. I've summoned you here to repay that favour you owe - Stop laughing." She cut off his bitter laugh. "You're bound by oath, Jamie. I want you to get me an audience with the King."

"Why do you want to speak to that monster? How could you even stand to be near him?" He snapped. Hester paused before answering, her words picked slowly at first before growing in fervour.

"Under his rule, your brother was refused help and work, arrested and killed for something he had no control over. Under his rule, my beloved was killed last month for the same reason. I've seen it happen to hundreds this last year, alone. And if they aren't killed, it's because they've fled to backwater villages or abandoned homes in the middle of nowhere only to hide for the rest of their lives from a country that wants them dead. They didn't ask for this, none of us have! I want justice." The earlier sympathy made sense now, Jamie realised. He forced himself to squash down the anger that had flooded him.

"You want justice... So what, you're going to kill him?" It was hard to keep the pain from his voice. Jamie was not a crier, not since he was a little boy, but even now he could feel the prickling of tears threatening to fall.

"There are far worse things than death, Jamie Brackett. But yes. I intend to kill the King." A shard of ice had lodged itself in the heart of Hester, Jamie could see it in her steeled gaze.

He took a deep breath. If Hester could keep it together, so could he. Perhaps it was the shock, or the distraction of the task he'd been set, Jamie couldn't be sure. He didn't want to linger on the reason anymore.

"I'm not high ranking. I'm just a cleaner, sometimes a scribe. I might be able to get you in, but it would take a while." Hester waved away his hesitations.

"Tonight is the annual ball celebrating the King's coronation. All members of nobility are expected to attend, along with members of the household staff. Families of both are also invited, if I'm not mistaken?" His eyes widened in surprise. It was true. The annual coronation ball was meant to be a celebration for the nobility and a sign of gratitude to the staff, hence the invitation being extended to family members as well. He hadn't had plans on going, so the event hadn't crossed his mind until now. It was a good idea. She'd clearly done some research.

Still, he couldn't help point out the glaring flaw.

"We look nothing alike. There's no way you could pass as family." At first he didn't understand the sly grin on Hester's lips.

"You'll have to pass me off as your betrothed. At least until we're past the palace guards. Once I'm inside, I'll take it from there, and your debt will be repaid." The dark blush had shot across his cheeks like an arrow, and Jamie looked anywhere but at her.

"I-if I agree... Then that's it? All I have to do is help you get in?" She nodded.

"I'll make sure you aren't implicated in what I do. I'd ask you to do me the kindness of burying Nikeet's bones if anything happens to me. But other than that, you'd be free." Jamie hesitated. Considering that she could have asked him to do literally anything to fulfil the favour he owed, this wasn't exactly difficult for him. He didn't have to go out of his way for it either.

"Do I have to stay? I don't think I can be around those people," Jamie mumbled, fighting back the twinge of his heart.

"You don't... But you'll miss the show." This time the smile had become cruel, lighting up Hester's entire face. Finally, he sighed in defeat.

"How long exactly have you been planning this?"

"A while."

"And what made you think I'd agree to it?"

"The debt you owe me... And I thought you would want justice as much as I do." They fell silent as Jamie finished the dregs of his tea.

"...Okay. I'll meet you here at eight." She nodded gratefully.

"It's a date."

~*~

At eight on the dot, Jamie arrived in a cheap-hired horse and cart he drove himself. He wore a black suit, trousers fraying at the hem, and the jacket was just a fraction too short at the arms. Hester climbed up to sit beside him, the sight of her sending a chill through his body. She'd found a long velvet-black dress that flowed like water about her. Black lace enclosed her upper-arms, shoulders and neck, and her hair was styled in elaborate curls. The dress ended with deep black gloves encrusted with silver to shape sparkling claws at her fingertips. Finally, she drew a mask as dark as shadow, shaped like a bird's skull, down over her face. It was nothing like the fashion of the times, large hooped skirts swaying with each step and tight, low bodices. This was an outfit designed to make a statement, to be a warning.

"...I see you got the memo of this year's theme."

"Like I said, I've been planning this for a while." Jamie clicked his tongue, chivvying the horse into a steady trot. He had so many questions, but anxiety stilled his voice.

"When we get in, I'm going to socialise." Her grimace at the thought was audible in her voice. "If you want to join me, you're welcome. But I understand if you want to avoid being seen with me. It might even be safer for you if you kept your distance." She hesitated, and without seeing her face, Jamie could tell there was more.

"Whatever it is, say it. Quick and clean," he murmured, whilst keeping his eyes firmly fixed on the road ahead.

"I don't intend to survive, Jamie. Things are going to happen very quickly once they start. It's going to escalate, and I'll understand if you hate me for what will happen after tonight. But if there's a part of you that understands I had no choice, or thinks I would be able to help after the ball starts rolling... On the seventh night after my burial, you should come to the grave and dig me up. My familiar will know the way." She ignored the blend of horror and disgust on his face. "It'll make sense when you do it... If you do it. I won't hold it against you if you don't. Just remember, seven nights." Jamie shook his head in disbelief.

"Honestly, I have no idea what you're talking about... Other than you're asking me to *dig up your rotting body*. You're aware how creepy that sounds?" A strange sound came out of her, and when Jamie glanced to the side, he realised it was the first time he'd ever heard Hester laugh.

"I think creepy doesn't even begin to describe the situation, Jamie. Besides, I'm a necromancer, my boundaries of creepy are very different to yours." He answered with a curt nod, holding back a small smile. Perhaps in another life they could have been real friends. He doubted they'd have that chance now.

Arriving at the palace, he hopped down to help Hester off the cart, handing the reins to a stable hand. Hester remained stiff and silent as he guided her up the steps, holding out his invitation to one of the servants on duty. They gestured to a side entrance to be used by attending staff.

The ceilings of the hall were high and vaulted, with golden leaves spiralling out from the tops of columns. Delicate sculpture and paint work decorated the ceilings and walls. The room was the pinnacle of wealth, and neither Jamie or Hester spared it barely a glance around. Once they were fully inside, Hester gently detached herself from his arm.

"You have two hours to decide if you'll stay or leave."

"What are you doing in two hours?" He demanded.

"I'm going to put on a show." She refused to answer any questions, instead gliding away. Jamie melted into the background of the celebrations. He held a single glass of wine, of which he didn't sip, occasionally managing small conversation with some of the other employees of the palace. Although all attendees wore masks, even Jamie had slipped on a simple red mask, one could easily see the difference between nobility and staff. Keeping to the outskirts of the hall, he avoided having to speak to nobility, doubted even that they knew he was there. This kind of invisibility allowed him to follow Hester's movements.

Jamie watched as Hester navigated her way through the dancing, giggling guests. Now and then she would pause to strike up conversation. He'd never known Hester to be overly fond of contact, yet he could see her hands lightly patting the shoulder of a gentleman, or squeezing the hand of a lady as her lips rang with bright laughter. It stoked the still glowing coals of his anger. How could she waste his time like this? She had promised him justice on the people who had taken his brother and countless others, yet here she was, wasting time. Without fully realising it, Jamie had made the decision to stay, and now the wait was excruciating.

Time ticked by slowly and Jamie grew bored of watching. Instead he turned to filling himself with free food, more sumptuous than anything he could afford. Wine and chatter with the few people he knew helped to eat away the time, and for a moment, Jamie found himself almost having fun.

Until a sound made his head whip up so fast his neck cracked. The great double doors had slammed open. The noble guests had enough time to step back to the sides of the room, as if they knew what was happening and were following well rehearsed steps, whilst those lower ranked scrambled to follow suit. A small figure appeared from the darkness outside, stumbling into the hall. Red prints marked where his bare and battered feet had stepped. His eyes were sunken and his clothes were rags, clinging to his frail, emaciated body. But what kept Jaime's attention was the mask clasped tightly around the boy's lower face, silencing any sound as he staggered forward, and the ties around his wrists and hands, binding them to prevent even the slightest twitch.

He recognised the bindings too well. The last time he'd seen them had been around his own brother's hands and mouth. Jamie didn't realise he'd dropped his glass, as the sharp snap of black boots marching in unison had filled the air, muffling the sound. Royal guards, in all their finery, proceeded in two long lines down the hall, forming a barrier between the onlookers and the lone Witch child. Once they were in place a final figure emerged, draped in more gold and sparkling gems than Jamie had ever seen. The King had arrived with a little sport.

The audience held their breath as the King raised an ornate crossbow. Balanced carefully in his arms, he took aim. The boy had time for one brief cry for help, before the arrow was loosed and lodged into his flesh.

His lungs gurgled and rattled with each strained breath he sucked in. His chest heaved with the effort, as dark red blood spread out around the broken body that had crumpled to the ground. It was no killing blow, but one aimed to cause pain and long-suffering misery. Cheers and rallying cries of joy and excitement burst around the hall. The thrill of the sport, the success of yet another Witch exterminated, pulsed through the noble audience. The King lowered his crossbow as he paraded about his court, basking in their praise.

At first no one noticed a darkly-dressed figure slipping out from the crowd and crouching beside the boy. No one saw the surprisingly gentle fingers rest against his forehead and chest. No one but the boy, who stared with pleading eyes. Eyes that clouded over in death moments later. It took a few seconds before one of the guards noticed the lack of sound from the boy and glanced over.

He raised the alarm with a sharp shout and whistle. When Hester straightened up, she peered about the room as, one by one, the guards raised their swords and bayonets to point in her direction, forming a bristling barrier between herself and the party guests.

"Well, this is quite the welcome." Her voice rang clear and confident through the stunned silence of the guests as she held her head high in defiance.

Hester raised her open hands slowly, and the guards took a step closer, tightening the circle around her. At least, they tried to. When they stepped in, Hester closed her hands into tight fists. A pulse rippled through the crowd, before people began to gasp and shout in alarm. Seven figures shoved past the armed guards, staggering with disjointed movements. They walked like puppets handled by an unskilled marionette, jerking with each step. While their bodies moved forwards to form a human shield about Hester, their eyes were wide with terror, mouths no longer open in laughter and jeers but in silent screams.

Jamie had tried to move closer to get a better view, to see and understand what Hester had been planning all along. Here he could see that the glint of her silvered 'claws' was dulled by a faint red sheen, and now her earlier 'friendly touches' made chilling sense. If a necromancer possessed someone's blood, they had the potential to control their body. As the living puppets settled into place, Jaime noticed that the body of the dead Witch child did not stir from its peaceful stillness.

For a few brief heartbeats no one spoke. No one breathed. The King himself was frozen at the audacity of a commoner. With a quick shake, he drew himself up to his full, perfectly average height, and gave Hester his most impressive royal stare. She raised a questioning brow.

"Stand down Witch." The King spat out the word as if it were the filthiest thing to have left his mouth.

"I don't think I will." The King struggled not to appear flustered at the calm, laid back air Hester was giving off. His attempts didn't last long when she began to take slow, measured steps towards him, her living shield shuffling with her. The King tried to step back, but there was nowhere for him to go. The crowd that had been so eager to watch his show had now become his barrier. Eyes wide in alarm, the King tried to snap out orders, and a brave guard lunged forwards to jab his sword between the bodies guarding Hester. She simply flicked a hand to the side, and one of the puppets let out a shrill cry of pain as they staggered to block the blade. Hester didn't spare the guard a look.

She continued to advance forward, until all that separated herself and the King was a single body. Jamie tried to lean in closer to hear what was being said. The King's voice was stammering but low, and he was blocked by Hester's shield, making it harder to hear his words. The crowd shifted and stirred, the atmosphere balancing on a knife edge between panic and rage. He wanted desperately to reach for her, to stand by her side and watch the death of the pathetic man who had so callously called for his brother's murder. But Jamie found himself frozen and muted. He couldn't bring himself to break the tension of the room.

Finally, Hester's voice rose above the discordant whispers. "King Aldrich. I have heard and seen enough. Whilst I never aspired to be a judge, juror or executor, it seems I must become all three tonight. On behalf of the souls of every Witch you have had killed, I declare you guilty. I sentence you to death by hand of the Witch. With this act, may my people rise from their ashes. And may you, and each of your followers, rot in hell." She spat the final words like a snake releasing its venom. No one had time to react.

As the guards lunged for Hester and her quivering shields, giving more care for the life of their King than those of her noble hostages, no one noticed the small figure rising from the pool of its own blood. No one watched as, with inhuman strength, it tore its hands free from the bindings. No one saw the dead little Witch as he punched his fist through the King's chest and crushed his panicking heart in an act of final revenge beyond the grave. All eyes had been on Hester, and no one noticed her final puppet until the inky redness spread across the King's chest. His glassy eyes were wide with surprise as he fell, to lie beside the once again motionless body of the small Witch child.

Jamie knew what would happen next. He didn't stay. Instead he turned and fled the screams of horror and fury, and the rattle of gun fire. He didn't see the bullets rip through the nobles that had protected Hester, until the guards had stopped caring for their lives. Jamie didn't watch as the blades were plunged into her proudly standing body. Nor did he notice that he was not the only one running. If he had paused, he would have seen, amidst the panicking nobles, a few of his fellow servants exchange knowing glances. Perhaps he would have spotted the glimmer of magic and purpose behind their gazes as, one by one, they slipped away to spread the news.

The King was dead. A revolution was about to begin.

Seven nights later, Jamie found himself in a small patch of land on the outskirts of Newton. It was barren, abandoned, and untouched by the fighting that had broken out across the city mere hours after King Aldrich's death. Abandoned, apart from himself and a small sparrow perched on his shoulder. The little bird had led him to this place, as it had always led him to where he was needed.

For hours, Jamie had dug under the unforgiving moon's stare, his sleeves rolled up high with sweat making the old grey shirt cling to his back. Finally he stood up, cracking his joints before pulling himself up out of the dark hole. He waited, crouched at the edge for a few moments, the sparrow nestled in his tightly curled hair. Neither spoke, only one breathed, and only the stars and moon observed their vigil, as fires flickered in the distance throughout the raging city. Finally, a hand, as pale and cold as Jamie had always known, reached up from the hole, and Jamie let out a gasping laugh. He reached out and grasped the other tightly, relief that his suspicions had been proven correct.

Death is but a small inconvenience to a Necromancer.

About the Author

A witch can be many things. Leeper has chosen to dedicate her time and magic to the chronicling of the history of her people. The real history. The side of history most don't get to hear. Her fascination began with the legend and tales that arose from the Shadow Wars. Her active interest in discovering these secret histories has sent her down many a winding path of adventure and exploration. When not on the hunt for such stories, she and her familiar spend their days relaxing in the Quiet Spaces, exploring New Frontiers, or else settling down with a good book. She specialises in weather magic, dabbling in curses, and consuming stories old and new.

The Unwanted Presence
By Arete B. Rogers

The house was quiet and dark. As far as Kate knew, she was the only one awake. She'd been lying in bed for the last few minutes, trying to decide whether she was thirsty enough to get a drink of water from the kitchen. The problem was she'd have to sneak downstairs in the dark to get it. She wasn't afraid of the dark. Not really. But she never liked being the only person up. The house always seemed... different at night, like it was a stranger's house. It was silly to think like that. It wasn't like houses took turns being inhabited by people. But still...

It's silly, she told herself, and she was starting to believe it. Treading softly, she crept out of her room and down the stairs. The house still felt different. And... The air was different. It felt like something had moved.

Kate's eyes went to the old wooden rocking chair in the corner. It had been part of the furniture when she and her mom had moved into the house and was the only thing they'd kept. She thought it looked like the chair had slowly come to a stop. The only thing definitely different about it was a half-folded newspaper. Usually, her mom cleaned up right before bed. Kate shrugged and went to pick up the paper. But as she came closer to the chair, the air grew colder. And it seemed there was a shadow on the chair. The shadow of a man.

Kate turned and fled the room. Even if being afraid of the dark was silly, it'd played on her too much. She went back to her room, closed the door, and crawled back into bed, wrapping the sheets tightly around her.

I don't like it. I don't care if there's nothing *there.*

The sad thing is, there really was.

~*~

Down in the living room was a ghost. He'd been there all night, keeping quiet and minding his business, and would have been very happy to have been be left that way. His name was Mr. Giles, and he'd been dead for almost three years.

Mr. Giles had arisen from his chair when the girl had seen his shadow. It was instinct to try to reassure the girl or explain himself, but it wouldn't have worked. He sighed and ran his hands through his hair. Even if she could see him, she wouldn't want to. In life he'd been a man about average height, with grey eyes and thick grey hair, and he looked exactly how he had when he'd died. This was a constant source of discomfort for him because he was nearly completely naked.

Mr. Giles had died one night in his favorite chair, wearing nothing but his red and white striped boxer shorts, and that's how he looked now as a spirit. He could've gotten out of this problem if he'd been laid to rest in better clothes, but it hadn't worked out that way. He'd barely had enough time to call the hospital from his cell phone, and by the time they'd arrived, he was dead. According to his will, he was cremated and, evidently, they decided not to waste money on a suit for a body that would go up in smoke.

To this day Mr. Giles grumbled to himself about how inconvenient death was, and how inconsiderate. People talked about a skeleton in a robe carrying a scythe coming for you, or a beautiful woman with black wings, but one thing it never did was give you some bloody advance notice! You know, give you time to set your affairs in order, call the funeral home, put some pants on!

His home and possessions had been auctioned off and, with nothing else to do, Mr. Giles had decided to just stay where he was. A middle-aged woman named Amy and her daughter Kate had moved in about a month after the auction. They were nice people. Kate didn't cause a mess, Amy kept everything neat and tidy, and she made French toast every morning. Mr. Giles loved going to sleep with that scent in the air, and was glad it one of the few things he could still do. For these reasons he didn't actively haunt them and kept to himself, comfortable knowing that there was a good woman keeping his carpets clean.

Mr. Giles tried to go back to his paper, but his heart just wasn't in it. He mulled over how he might make it up to Kate, but nothing came to mind. He couldn't talk to anyone unless they had some talent for the supernatural, and as far as he could see, neither of the women did. They had a cousin named Sam who stopped by sometimes, and who seemed to have an air of the mystic about him. However, Mr. Giles chose to rest during the day and turn the house over to the girls, so he knew very little about cousin Sam.

After a few hours sitting, Mr. Giles rose from his chair and floated to the window. He wanted to watch the neighbors. They were usually out by now. Yes, there was old Mrs. Fitz, floating next to the Rodriguez couple, talking animatedly with them beneath the nearest street lamp. Across the street was Gabby, the Henderson's old poodle, happily chasing her tail. She was able to catch it much more easily now she'd been cut in half by the wheel of a speeding car. The Rodriguezes and Mrs. Fitz smiled and waved at Mr. Giles, and he heartily waved back.

Unlike Mr. Giles, the average ghost liked to get out of the house, shake off the dust and cobwebs and get some air. They'd float around to places they'd visited in life and meet with other dearly departed friends to pass the time. Upon dying, Mr. Giles had had a visit from a few of the locals, ready with a handshake to welcome him to the "Post-Fatality Fraternity" as they called it. The consensus among the spirits of the neighborhood seemed to be that being stuck in underwear was like a stammer or a birthmark; you could look past it and the more you got to know the person, the less their condition mattered. Mr. Giles had accepted their welcome, but he never socialized much in life, and it was a hard habit to break now, even without the problem of his wardrobe.

Realizing that he was conspicuous at the window, Mr. Giles turned to float into another room before coming to an abrupt halt. A creeping feeling had come over him, like a sudden realization that something bad he'd overlooked was now apparent. But it wasn't something he'd found, it was something felt. From outside. If he'd had breath it would have caught in his throat.

He went back to the window and looked out at the street. Mr. and Mrs. Rodriguez, Mrs. Fitz, and the dog had all frozen in what they were doing. He made eye contact with Mrs. Fitz, and saw her eyes were wide, and her shoulders drawn back. Mr. Giles shrugged and raised his hands.

There was a flash of light at the end of the block. The ghosts turned toward it and saw a misty form appear under a lamppost. It wasn't ghostly white or grey, but black. Blacker than the night, and the yellow light of the street lamp didn't show through it. It looked human, but bigger in the head and around the shoulders, and it looked like it had three legs. Gabby the dog started barking. Her front half bounced with each bark while her back half trembled. The person –if that's what it was– made a clawing gesture in the air, then turned and crossed the street. The poor dog yipped and ran out of sight.

The spirits on the near side of the street turned and floated away as fast as they could, but Mr. Giles could only stand and watch as it came closer. As it approached, he saw that what he'd at taken for a third leg was actually a thick, scaly tail.

The thing crossed the sidewalk, and then came up to the door of the house. It was almost six feet tall and dark red. It wore no clothing but a loin cloth. Its bald head was almost twice the size of a normal human's head, and crowned with two sharp five-inch horns above its small, pointed ears. Its face was human, with reptilian eyes and thin lips. Its gaze roved over the house, and it smiled. Its teeth were large, even for a head that size. It had canines like tusks on its upper and lower jaw, and its front teeth were at least two inches wide and three long.

Its arms –long enough to touch its scaly knees– folded over its thin chest. It smiled a wide, gratified smile, which reminded Mr Giles of the guy in his old office who'd bragged about how important his position was. With one taloned hand, it reached for the doorknob.

Click.

Mr. Giles made a move to hold the door closed before he remembered that, as a ghost, his strength was limited to moving small objects. He couldn't stop that thing from coming into his home, and if he'd still had a heart, it would've been hammering.

The thing put one long, clawed foot slowly over the threshold. It bent over to clear the doorframe and grinned widely. As the thing crossed the foyer, the door creaked closed. Mr Giles heard it lock itself again.

The creature seemed taller inside the house than it had outside. It laughed, a laugh like the voice of a ghost, not heard but sensed. In its case, it sounded like the voice that tells you to kill the person you hate.

The thing took a breath, rising to its full, tremendous height.

"I am Garol-"

THUNK.

Its head bumped the ceiling.

The creature touched its right horn, which had lost its sharp point. It turned its head sideways to look up at the ceiling. It huffed, and hung its head between its shoulders, as it began to speak again.

"I am Garoldyne, Junior Prince of Hell. This home, and all who live in it, I claim as MY cattle, under the authority of my father, Iblis the Terrible."

A shudder ran through the air. It touched Mr. Giles, and he felt unclean.

"Alright. That's it," he said.

The demon turned at the sound of his voice. Mr. Giles folded his arms over his chest and took another step into the living room.

"Pardon me. You're in my home, sir. And-" he said, with more bravado than he felt, "–I believe you've just scratched my ceiling."

The demon turned to Mr. Giles. Its claws flexed as it spoke again.

"I am Garoldyne! Garoldyne the Cruel! Garoldyne the Tormentor! I feed on the hearts of children and drink the tears of those lost in the night! My song is the lament of mothers! I am Garoldyne! And I claim this house as MY property! And YOU, human, shall have the honor of being my FIRST victim!"

It lunged at him. Mr. Giles had only a second to take in the dark face and yellow teeth before it was on him.

Then in him. Then through him, followed by the body, legs, and tail.

THUD!

It'd launched itself through his ghostly body and hit the wall.

The demon stood again and touched its head. Now both of its horns had been dented and bore a stronger resemblance to bent thumbs.

"Oh. You're a phantom," said the demon.

"Yes. I would've thought the being all pale and see-through would've made that obvious."

The demon puffed itself up in indignation.

"I THOUGHT you might've been astral projecting! Then I could've cut the cord to your mortal form, and KILLED you!"

Mr. Giles leaned against the wall.

"Your dramatic presentation is remarkable. Did I see you in a cartoon when I was a kid?"

The demon's face twisted into a sneer, and his eyes burned red. "Ohhhhhh. You'd be DEAD if you were alive!"

Mr. Giles blinked. He was safe, but the girls upstairs...

He swallowed and continued. "If I had boots I'd be shaking in them, Mr. Devil. Now, if you don't mind, I'm sure you've woken up everyone in the house!"

The demon stood as tall as the ceiling would allow him. "I am Garoldyne! Juni-" he cut himself off "PRINCE of Hell! And I shall claim the souls of women who live here!"

Mr. Giles cocked an eyebrow. "Tell me Gargler, what's a Junior Prince of Hell?"

Garoldyne's face flushed even darker red. "I need not talk to you! They approach!"

Now Mr. Giles heard it. Footfalls on the stairs. He felt the place where his stomach had been drop.

He saw Amy at the foot of the stairs, looking wide-eyed around the dark living room, a pistol in her hand. But even if she could see in the dark, the demon was as invisible as Mr. Giles.

The demon leered at Mr. Giles and began to murmur.

"One… Two… Satan's coming for you."

Amy froze. The ghost of Mr Giles saw her turn pale. "Who? Wh-h-ho's i-in here? I-I'm armed."

Garoldyne's smile widened. "It's a pity she can't see me," he said. He began to sneak across the room.

"Three. Four. Never sleep no more."

"Is that your big shtick?" Mr. Giles asked. "Just rip off horror movies?"

The demon pursed his lips but kept his eyes on Amy.

"Mind the pillow on the floor."

Garoldyne tried to pause mid-step and check his footing, and almost lost his balance. His foot landed harder than he'd intended and made a small sound. Amy turned her pistol to the point where the sound had come from. Now it was the demon who froze.

And then, Mr. Giles had an idea. He floated over to the couch and stuck his ghostly hand into the cushions. He felt the demon's eyes on his back and he threw a wave over his shoulder.

Straightening, he pulled out a small, dirty penny. He floated over to Amy and grinned. "Saw a trick like this in a movie once," he said.

He brought the penny to the trigger of the gun, and before Garoldyne knew what was happening, used the coin to squeeze Amy's finger on the trigger.

BANG!

Amy screamed as the bullet plowed through Garoldyne's left shoulder. He fell to the ground in a spray of dark blood where he clutched at the wound. His yowl of pain reverberated off the walls and through the house.

From the top of the steps came a shriek. "Mom!"

Garoldyne looked to the top of the steps, and then back to Mr. Giles. The demon's face changed from pain to glee. He bolted past both the ghost of Mr. Giles and Amy, knocking the woman to the floor. He flew up the stairs, to where Kate stood, wide-eyed.

Garoldyne looked back down the stairs. "I saw THIS in a movie once!" His hand passed into the girl's head. Kate's eyes bulged, her arms twitched, her mouth stretched in a silent scream.

"Kate?" called Amy. "Kate!?" She clutched her face in horror.

Garoldyne rocked Kate back and forth, and Mr. Giles could see muscles tighten in the creature's arm. Kate closed her mouth. He tensed again, and she blinked.

"Hello, mother," said the demon and girl together. But it wasn't Kate's voice coming from her mouth, but a deep, savage growl. Kate's face paled before the eyes of her mother and Mr. Giles. Her hair rose like the hackles of a cat, and her wide, bulging eyes drained of color along with her skin.

"Katie! My God! What's wrong?!"

The demon cackled through the girl's mouth.

"It's not Kate anymore! Hee hee hee! Her soul is MINE!"

Mr. Giles tried to keep his cool. There was a window at the end of the hall, and he could see the sky slowly turning pink. Maybe demons had to follow rules like ghosts did. Maybe he could keep it distracted. It should probably be easy.

"Oh dear," said the ghost. "What a terrible fate. Her soul is claimed by Hell's junior executive."

Both the demon and the girl growled.

"I suppose that means she'll be condemned to an eternity of fetching coffee and taking memos. Truly that is Hell."

"Shut up," said the demon and girl.

"What?" Amy said.

"Not you! Him!" Garoldyne twisted his arm, and Kate pointed down the stairs to where Mr. Giles stood, invisible, next to Amy.

"Kate?" Said Amy. She was slowly climbing the stairs, the gun abandoned on the landing below her. "Kate? What's wrong baby? What's happened to your eyes?"

Kate and Garoldyne snarled and began to walk backwards to the wall. Amy quickened her pace, followed by Mr. Giles.

At the wall, the demon pulled up with the spectral hand in Kate's head. Without taking her eyes off her mother, she put both hands and feet on the wall and began to climb it like a spider. She laughed in a sick, sputtering, phlegmy gurgle. "She's MIIIIINE now woman! With her soul, I shall rise in the underworld, and become greater and more powerful!"

The demon's back was to the window. He hadn't noticed the sky changing color. "What's next? Middle-management?" asked the ghost of Mr. Giles. "It's a shame really. The son of a great demon and you need to bring in outside help to help you climb the ladder. He mustn't be that terrible after all."

Garoldyne and Kate snarled again. "For your information, he could get me any entry-level position I wanted! I just wanted to make my OWN way!"

"By copying the Exorcist?"

"SHUT UP!" yelled the demon and the girl together. Her breaths quickened and became more shallow. Her shoulders heaved, her throat bulged like a bullfrog's, and a torrent of brown and pink slime spewed from her mouth and nose. Amy screamed and slipped back down the stairs, bracing herself against the wall to stop her head from hitting it.

The demon laughed. "My goodness."

"My BABY!"

"MY CARPET!"

The landing now reeked of vomit and half-digested food. Garoldyne laughed through his slave again and began to chant.

"One! Two! Satan's coming for you!"

"Seven, eight, nine, ten," Mr. Giles said.

"Seven! Ei- Wait, no! Two, three- DAMMIT!" The red eyes of the demon were fixed on Mr. Giles. The hand over his wound was clenched in a bloody fist, and his fangs were bared. Kate's back arched. She was coughing as she breathed, gobs of vomit running from her nose.

"Why don't you come back tomorrow night and get some original material! You look like you could use a good day's sleep!" Mr. Giles pointed to the window, where the clouds had gone from pink to flaming orange.

The demon looked. He hissed through his and Kate's teeth, and let the girl fall to the floor, into the puddle of her own vomit. Amy screamed again and ran back up the stairs to her daughter.

"I WILL be back, ghost!" the demon said, pointing to Mr. Giles with the hand that had been covering his bullet wound. It was still slick with his blood. "Mock me all you want, you've only increased my fury!"

He backed into a shadowy corner, as far from the creeping golden light as he could get. He became less and less distinct from the wall, almost like a ghost himself. "I have all day to plan what I'll do next. Maybe I'll make her eat cockroaches. Hmm? Or shove her down the stairs? Or better yet, throw her out that window! I am Garoldyne! And I will be back tonight!"

The demon faded from sight, leaving only a damp smoky scent, and an echoing laugh.

Mr Giles didn't disappear like the demon had with the rising sun. Instead, he just faded a bit. Not quite there, and not quite gone. It was like staying up way too late, with events blurring together in a haze.

He saw Amy make a hurried phone call, and a short time later, paramedics rushed into the house. They took Kate away on a stretcher as Amy was interviewed by a police officer.

He watched Amy try to clean up the mess on the second floor. She kept stopping to look at her cell phone, and once or twice her shoulders heaved - whether from crying, or trying to keep from throwing up herself, Mr. Giles couldn't tell.

She called to check in on her daughter three times, and each time she hung up after just a few seconds with whoever was on the line. Then around noon he saw her call again and heard the name, Sam. She talked on the phone for a few minutes, and when she hung up, she went straight into her room. She came out again with a small blue travelling case, got into her car, and drove away.

That evening Mr. Giles was in his rocking chair again. He couldn't call the hospital, and he didn't know what Amy's number was. Not that it would do any good anyway.

The ghost of Mr. Giles tried to float around the living room to clear his head. He tried to let go of the knot of worry in his stomach, but couldn't. He could do nothing about his fear, his worry for the girls or his nerves about the demon's return except prepare himself. He couldn't touch it. But... It couldn't touch him either. And, as if the thought of the damned thing had summoned it, he felt something in the air. It wasn't the forlorn, cold sensation of another ghost. It was darker. Garoldyne came through the door again, and saw Mr. Giles, alone in the living room.

"Hello, ghost," the demon said.

Mr. Giles sighed. "Oh, crap. You did come back."

Garoldyne smirked. "You dreaded my return, little ghost?"

Mr. Giles jerked a thumb back up to the second floor. "Do you have any idea how much it costs to rip up a carpet?"

The demon's grin dropped. Whatever he'd expected, that wasn't it.

"You drop in in the middle of the night uninvited, raise an uproar, climb the walls and leave a mess on the carpet. You sir, are bad company."

"I am a prince of Hell!"

"And you clearly skipped an etiquette class!"

The demon bared his teeth and seethed with anger, and Mr Giles felt the temperature in the room rise.

Mr. Giles squared his shoulders. "Now would you kindly piss off?"

Garoldyne's voice came as a growl. "This house and its living inhabitants are mine. I have so many ideas for what to do with that girl, and her dear, dear mother."

"Oh. Like what?"

"I will make the girl eat cockroaches. I'll carve the name of my father into the skin of her arms." Garoldyne rubbed his claws together. "I'll pin her to the ground and spin her mother around on the ceiling! I'll-" The demon noticed the ghost looking at a painting on the wall. "Excuse me!"

"Hmm? Oh. I'm sorry. I don't really care, so I wasn't listening. Could you do me a favor and not repeat it?"

Garoldyne growled. "For that, I'll make this whole house ring with the screams of that sweet, tender child."

"Well, could you come back later? They're probably asleep by now."

"Ohhh." The demon purred. "But that's how I like my girls. Peaceful, innocent, and unsuspecting." He walked through the ghost and climbed silently up the stairs.

He stopped on the landing, raised his head and sniffed like a dog. His eyes fell on the door to Kate's bedroom.

Gently, he rested his hand on her doorknob and rattled it, enough to make the faintest of sounds. The demon smiled and rattled the handle again, more loudly.

He brought his other hand to the door, curling his fingers into a fist.

KNOCK. KNOCK. KNOCK.

He chuckled as he rattled the handle again, and this time, turned it all the way. The door opened with a soft creak. With one last look down the stairs at the ghost of Mr. Giles, the demon pushed his head into the room.

He looked around. He looked again. He pushed his whole head and shoulders into the room. He took his hand off the doorknob and turned the light on. Then he turned it off. He pulled his head back and looked down at Mr. Giles, who stood impassively at the foot of the stairs.

"She's not in there," the demon said.

"You don't say.."

"Where is she?"

The ghost of Mr. Giles rolled his eyes.

Garoldyne scowled, but crept to the next door. Slowly, he turned the handle and pushed the door wide open, letting it squeak.

He flicked the light on, snorted, and flicked it off. He went to the door on the other side of the landing and opened it. Nothing in the guest bedroom. Mr. Giles had to bite his lip to keep his reaction in.

Nothing in the bathroom.

Nothing in the hall closet.

Garoldyne came back to the top of the stairs and glared at Mr. Giles. "WHERE. ARE. THEY?!"

"They both left several hours ago." And Mr. Giles erupted in a fit of laughter.

"Ohhh!" Roared the demon. "If I could kill you I would kill you!"

"Oh-ho! Likewise!" Mr. Giles said. "You're a positive nuisance in this neighborhood!"

Garoldyne roared so loudly he shook the pictures on the walls. "I AM GAROLDYNE! I AM THE FIFTEENTH SON OF IBLIS THE TERRIBLE! I WILL NOT BE MOCKED BY YOU, GHOST!" A pungent stench like burned sewage filled the house. Garoldyne's skin darkened to the color of charcoal, and further to midnight black. He turned into a cloud of smoke and flew back down the stairs, and out into the night. Mr. Giles floated to the window to watch him go.

The black cloud hung over the street like a darker patch of night, rumbling. As it rose higher into the air, Mr. Giles could hear the voice of the Garoldyne.

"PHANTOM! MARK MY WORDS! I SHALL NOT LEAVE THIS WORLD WITHOUT THE SOULS OF THE WOMEN WHO SHARE YOUR HOME! WHEN NEXT I RETURN, ONE OF THEM WILL DIE!"

Mr. Giles shuddered. He hadn't felt dread like this since the night three years ago when he felt his heart stop.

~*~

The next morning, a car pulled up in the driveway. The door opened and a man stepped out. The man was Sam, and he was carrying a wooden cross and a black bag.

Sam unlocked the door with a key and stepped cautiously inside. He looked around as if expecting someone or something to be lurking in a corner. He sniffed the air, and quickly covered his nose.

Carefully, he crept across the living room and up the stairs. In the light of day, he could see a discoloured spot on the landing. He shuddered and stepped around it into Kate's room.

Sam laid down on the bed, taking deep breaths, quieting his thoughts. He imagined his soul rising from his body, like crawling out of a warm bath. As he went he got deeper and deeper into relaxation. His body began to vibrate. Slowly the vibrations subsided, and he felt his body and his spirit as two different things. Connected, but distinct. Floating in the air, he began to search the room.

He found nothing in Kate's room, so he floated to Amy's room, then the other rooms, but to no avail.

Undeterred, he floated down to the first floor. At the foot of the staircase, he froze. There, in the corner rocking chair, was a shirtless man with his hands folded in his lap, and one leg crossed over the other.

"Hello," said Mr. Giles. He didn't speak with sound, but Sam heard.

"H-Hello."

"Yes, I'm a ghost. Dennis Giles. Nice to meet you."

"Hi. I'm-" Sam cut himself off. If this ghost was connected to Kate's haunting, he didn't want to risk giving his own name out. "…Kate and Amy's cousin."

"Yes. I kno-" Mr. Giles tried to hide a yawn behind a transparent hand. "Sorry. I've been worried about that poor girl and her mother so much, I haven't had a good day's sleep in ages." He sat a little straighter in the chair, still keeping his legs crossed. "You're one of those… mediums, aren't you? I've seen shows about people like that on late night television."

"Uh, yes. Um, are you the original owner of this house?"

"Yes, I am." Mr. Giles smiled. "Altogether I've been on this earth about fifty-three years. I'm quite fond of your cousins for how they've taken care of my home."

"OH!" Sam brightened and gave a genuine smile. "I'm glad to hear that. It's because of them that I'm here."

Mr. Giles nodded. "That demon, right? Ugly little thing, and stupid to boot. I've tried to do my best against him, but I'm afraid all I can do is take the piss out of him."

"Please, Mr. Giles. I need to know, have you, by any chance, learned the demon's name?"

"Oh yes. He keeps proclaiming it as if it'll impress me."

If Sam still had a physical mouth, it would've gone dry. "Please Mr. Giles. Dennis. I need to know its name. If I know it, I can control it and send it out of this house forever."

"Oh!" Said Mr. Giles, and he uncrossed his legs, leaning closer. "Is that how it works? I never knew!"

Sam felt wild hope rise in what would have been his chest. "Yes, sir. Please, tell me his name!"

Mr. Giles opened his mouth, and faltered. "Uhmmm."

"You do know, yes?"

"Yes. It's just... I was... Thinking... Nevermind. His name is Garoldyne."

There was a shift in the air around them. It was the feeling of eyes on the back of your head. Sam felt that something had heard its name.

Sam and Mr. Giles froze. The feeling seemed to sweep through the house, and over them. Sam reached out to his body. In an emergency, he could pull himself back in, and he prepared to do so.

"Excuse me," said Mr. Giles.

"What?"

"I was... Wondering if you could help me with something. You see, I... have a problem."

Sam looked around. "What is it?"

~*~

Sam left the house briefly after his meeting with Mr. Giles, returning in the afternoon with a large grey bag. He stayed in the house all day, reading a small black book. At six o'clock he set the book down and rolled out a large piece of paper. On it he drew a star, enclosed in a circle. As dusk fell, he felt a presence come into the house. Something evil. Quickly, he began to chant:

"In the name of the Lord, the Father Almighty who made Sea and Earth and Heaven, in the name of Jesus Christ, His Son, and through the power of the Holy Spirit, I cast out the demon from this house. I send you back to hell, demon Garoldyne!"

He hadn't opened any doors or windows, but Sam felt a wind whip through the room, and in the wind he could clearly hear two voices. One was a wild, anguished scream, and the other a man yelling:

"AND STAY OUT!"

The wind died, and the house was still.

Sam sighed and rolled up the paper with the pentagram. Then, he rolled out another piece of paper, and drew another circle, this time with a cross in it. Over the cross he laid the bag, so the logo Murphy's Apparel was displayed prominently. He picked up the black book and read aloud from it. When he'd finished and looked down at the circle, the bag was empty.

Sam spent the rest of night lighting incense in every room and touching the lintels of every door with holy water. When he was satisfied, he crawled onto the couch and slept.

The late morning sun woke him. He opened the windows on the ground and second floors, letting the last of the incense waft out with the breeze. He fixed himself a sandwich in the kitchen and called Amy.

That night Amy and Kate returned home to find Sam waiting at the front door, and they were escorted into the kitchen to find a full dinner laid out for them.

The ghost of Dennis Giles left the family to their meal, content to lean back in his chair and listen to his houseguests talk late into the night. Amy and her daughter were safe, the house was protected, and he had a new suit of proper clothes.

Ask anyone who's ever been alive and they'll tell you, it's the little things that matter.

About the Author

In this story you'll find an account of a terrible possession and an annoying haunting. Terrors abound, including a hellish junior executive and the ghost of a man trapped forever in his boxer shorts.

This tale of supernatural beings and subpar intelligence is sure to keep you hooked as the dead and the never-living vie for the fates of a family in a battle of wit and half-wit. Join us in this tale of the Unwanted Presence.

Phantoms at Glenkos
By Matty Hughes

I remember not why our venture into the south had brought us to the abnormal city that is Glenkos. The undesired effects of the cloaked figure's touch had yet rendered my memory somewhat unattainable to anything before our arrival here.

I do yet retain the idea that we came here through the means of horse and carriage and that myself and my partner Adam, had been attempting to sell some form of goods. However, as clever as we had been as salesmen before we came here, our charismatic sales pitches had clearly not appeased the people of this city. For I now find myself trapped and chained in a run down cellar beneath the ground. The bars of my cell seem corroded, but the strength of a starved man would not be enough to bend apart the bars that refused me my freedom. The townsfolk say soon I will be freed, but their rather unsympathetic tone suggests they have other intentions for my life.

We travelled to the city using some rather desolate countryside roads. I recall Adams surprise at the lack of activity we had encountered during our journey. Neither man nor wildlife bothered us.

The roads were dead.

While this would usually be a good sign back west, one can easily take pleasure in knowing he's not the only living soul this far east. When we finally did make it to the city, the entrance lacked any form of guard or protection. In fact the gate was not a gate, but rather a stone arch big enough to allow a carriage to pass through with ease. For a city of this scale, so far from any other inhabited land and with an allegiance to no other kingdom, one would think a gate would have been put in place to protect its citizens from mountains bandits or wandering wildlife.

Once inside, however, we came across something even more bizarre about the city. Down every narrow corner and city square would stand rather tall, hooded figures. Their black robes and drooping hoods must have made it impossible to retain any clear vision. This in itself was not too odd, as when travelling through the deserts of Nihrin one encounters a variety of different monks and cultists, all donning some rather interesting and unique garments. However, these figures had on robes that were almost impossible for the eye of a man to properly comprehend. It was not as if the men, or perhaps woman, were transparent, and I do not speak of men who are too bright to look at. Rather the silent, hooded entities that roamed the streets and alleyways of this otherwise normal city wore clothing of such a dark, black richness that actually trying to look at the robes would confuse the mind. It was as if some sort of optical illusion was being performed by a festival street performer. It had taken Adam and I quite a while to truly grasp what it was that we were seeing, and after nearly 25 minutes of discussion and debate, we gave up trying to figure out what they were and continued with our day, trying to ignore the strange men as they walked past us, and taking note of how they paid no attention to anything or anyone around them.

We set our carriage up just on the outskirts of the market place. It had just struck mid-day and the market place of Glenkos was flourishing with city life. The city itself stood on the support of stone made from compressed and hardened sand. This gave the city an almost yellow glow when hit by the sun's light. This colour contrasted nicely with the dark green of our carriage and combined with Adam's ever so convincing sales pitch, it drew a large number of happy customers for the day.

When we first started to sell our goods, I referred a few times to our customers about the conversation Adam and I had been having on the hooded figures, hoping to gain some answers on the nature of these mysterious creatures. Doing so only unsettled me more, however, as most of the townspeople seemed taken aback by the question and would either ask for further details or act as if I were mad. None of the citizens of this city retained any knowledge on these creatures that stalked the alleyways of their own city. It was as if everyone else were blind to these things except Adam and me. When we spoke later, he claimed to have had the same experience with the people he had served and it was then that we made the decision to leave the following morning. We would take the money we had gained and use it to buy a stock of food that would hopefully keep its freshness until we could pass through the narrow valley and back into Skirn. We did not know why we frightened so easily, but our instincts had kept us going for this long, and therefore we had learnt to trust them when it came to feelings of our own safety. I recall, during the night, looking out of the inn room's window to see the hooded figures had not stopped their patrol of the city. Their feet covered by their robes, they swept silently through the streets. There was always at least one in every main street and more in the alleyways. Although they never seemed to pay notice to anything, the creatures appeared to have no goal or objective. This did not put my mind to rest and I got little sleep that night.

The sun had barely finished rising when we left the city that following morning. The heat of the sun proved rather intense and so Adam and I took turns driving the carriage while the other rested inside. When noon hit us during our journey, we stopped at the side of the road and began to prepare our food for dinner. It was at this moment that Adam lifted the woven rug sack with our vegetables and pulled out a small silver blade. He then decided that then was the best time to reveal to me that the insignificant little item had belonged to one of the customers I had been serving. He had taken it from their belt while they had been observing our goods. This put me in a foul mood.

Adam had promised me several times his thieving days were done, only to disappoint me each time. I marched off into the carriage, furious at him, and ate my meal there before settling myself for the night and eventually falling into a sleep. He had claimed that it was necessary to keep us fed, but I knew Adam had done it for the sensational rush he had explained to me in-depth multiple times during our travels together.

I wish now we had never travelled east, to the sandstone city of Glenkos, for that night the carriage was visited by the most remarkable and unforgettable sight of blood and gore.

Though my memory is fleeting, I recall Adam's screams. I can't forget how he roared and whined. Like a child from the womb, he cried and he bled until he could cry no more. A large, frightening crunch was what finally stopped his movement as an enormous, decaying bony hand emerged from the black robed figure and wrapped itself around his bloody head like a parchment and tightened furiously. Adam's body had been dragged from the carriage and assaulted by three of the hooded figures we had seen in the city. These beings showed no mercy as they tore him apart like bloodthirsty hounds. As two of the figures approached me, the last thing I remember from that night was looking just behind them, to see the third creature begin to devour Adam's body, its back turned to me.

I awoke in this cellar and have been here for the last several days. I know not exactly how long I have been here, although I may guess I have been here at least three days. My stomach grumbles furiously, begging me for sustenance. The woman who comes to visit me three times a day sometimes leaves me the small leftovers of her own meals or some moulded bread she has no further use for. Sometimes a man comes in too. He always tells me to be quiet and to let him have a look at me. For what, I don't know, but I pray for my physical well-being, as well as my sanity. As the boredom and paranoia of my trapped, hunger driven mind is starting to tear me apart. I worry that if I don't get out soon, I will truly lose all recollection of who I am.

How long would I be kept here? Another week? A few weeks? A month?

~*~

Two days have passed.

The door to the cellar swings open revealing two men in strange, orange garments that hold short wooden sticks with curves on the side. They accompany the man and woman who have been visiting me the past week. I question who they are and what is happening but they tell me to be calm and that I will be free soon. They begin to open the door to my cell. I fall to my knees and thank them; the idea of me finally leaving this place fills me with a blessed joy I never thought I could experience. I imagine going as far away as possible from the accursed city of Glenkos, to never have to return.

When the cell door opened, however, the men in orange grab me by each arm and pin me against the wall. Their wooden instruments had been made to fit in a painful, tight embrace around my arms and keep me from escaping. From the doorway, one of the black hooded creatures emerges.

I struggle, I truly do.

I struggle with all the force I can muster. I struggle against the pain the wooden instruments cause me, and against the force of the men in orange robes. I have never been more petrified of anything as much as I am of the idea that I could possibly encounter one of these beasts again. And now reality is entertaining that possibility.

My weak, starved body is unable to free me from the weight of the men, as the black beast approaches me and takes a hold of my face with his bony, decaying hand. My flesh begins to burn away and corrodes from the bone. My skull, as well as my limbs, are engulfed in pain I had never thought possible. The pain spreads to my entire body and I scream and roar as my skin continues to disintegrate from the figure's touch. A thick, dark red stream of light spins around me like a strip of silk and the cloaked figure slowly strips me of myself.
He is conjoining his soul with mine. My last thought I remember…
Blood magic!

About the Author

In the east lies the city of Glenkos. A shinning glare in a barren land full of nightmares and terrors waiting for the unsuspecting traveller.

A Many-Faced Memory
by Kathryn Solly

Run. Just run, boy.
Why won't you run?
For the love of Helm just RUN, or we're both going to die here!

A sliver of silver cut the fabric of the darkness surrounding two figures, and the already drawn blade of a long hunting knife rose to meet it.

The taller figure wasn't sure why she'd chosen this form for the job, but she knew that no matter what forms she'd taken in the past, all of them would mean nothing if she didn't act quickly. The situation had got out of hand.

Her light, brown leather armour hugged her too tightly, the thin black clothing beneath it hiding every inch of skin. Half of her face was covered, leaving only the dark brown of her eyes glaring out from above her sharp cheekbones. Short, jaw-length hair hair danced in dark curls in the breeze of her recent movement, threatening to reveal the pointed tips of her copper-skinned elven ears.

The young boy behind her trembled, his knees weak with fear, the tiny dagger she had given him wavering in his hands.

When he had first called upon her for protection at the temple of Helm, she had debated whether or not to leave the boy to his fate. She wasn't sure on harbouring a criminal, but he was only a boy, after all.

Besides, the boy would suffer greatly for stealing a potion, and a pretty damn good one at that, the price of which would've been way above anything he would have been able to afford in the entirety of his poor lifetime. And the boy had used the potion to cure his dying mother, an act of compassion that was so rare to see in the world, and had felt guilt enough at stealing that he'd wanted to apologise and offer his unpaid servitude in exchange for his crime. How could she say no to protecting him until the shopkeeper had given him an answer? A pure heart was hard to come by these days. She had believed there was still time to set him on the right path.

However, the moment the shopkeep had seen him, a portly human that she had underestimated the speed of, the man had come at them in a squealing rage, sword withdrawn as he sought to claim his own justice.

She'd managed to get the boy away from the shop, but the evening had fallen quiet. There was nothing to cover them except the oncoming darkness as the shopkeep bore down on them.

Reaching the dead end of one of the city's alleyways, the two had turned back to face the shopkeep, but she couldn't talk their way out of it.

Speak and she'd be known.

Speak and she'd be remembered.

One word and she could be hunted down, and all those who needed her help would be lost to the corruption that she'd watched filter through the city for so many long years.

As steel clashed upon steel with a screech of metal as the blades slid against one another, the dagger dropped from the boy's hands and clattered to the street below and behind her. The sound startled his protector and for a split second her attention wavered from her opponent to the dagger as it bounced across the interlocked cobbles of the alley.

It was the opening the shopkeep had waited for.

He lunged, his face becoming visible in the light of the nearby brazier for all of a few seconds as he disengaged her blade and darted towards the boy, his own sword outstretched and gleaming.

Sensing her opportunity, she lunged for the shopkeep with her hunting knife, but was surprised to see the man lean out of the way as if having expected the move. He was no mere shopkeep, but she had realised too late. Mid-lunge, there was nothing she could do as the sword in his hand drove into the boy's stomach with a sickening squelch of ripping flesh, accompanied by the boy's agonised scream.

"No!" She yelled, turning back and staring, frozen in shock like a statue.

The shopkeep released the sword the moment it struck home, leaving the blade buried deep in the young boy's stomach. Now, he stepped towards her with his fist already raised, and his chapped, slightly split lips bearing a terrifying snarl.

"Protecting filth? What a joke."

The ring on his finger glinted in the firelight, a tiny sigil engraved into it, and it was the last thing she saw before pain exploded in the left side of her head, causing the world to cut to black.

~*~

When Eira awoke, she felt the soft sheets of the bed shift beneath her, it's silky smooth material brushing against her skin as she opened her eyes to see a beautiful white ceiling above her, patterned like a white and cream chessboard. The sharp tang of garlic spiked her senses and woke her fully.

She sat up suddenly, her hands clasping the sheets around her and pulled them tight to her in panic, but every movement seemed to send a jolt of pain shooting through her, sapping her of strength. All she could do was gasp as she spied the human male sitting in a large ornate chair beside her bed, asleep.

The gasp woke him, a startled expression crossing his face before he leaned forward, one hand rubbing his chin whilst the palm of his other hand faced her to caution her.

"Hey, hey, hey. Woah, wait."

She stared at him mutely until he rested his hands on his knees, staring back at her. He took a deep breath and she watched intently as he gazed at her, his light blue eyes evidently unsure of where to look as a small blush crept over his pale cheeks. His messy, dark brown shoulder length hair flowed over a dusted orange tunic, though half of his hair had been pulled back into a tight ponytail.

She noted scars down his left arm, the skin of which was horribly burnt and twisted where it hadn't healed properly. As though sensing what she was looking at, the strange man pulled the long sleeves of his tunic down from where they'd been rolled up to his elbows. She caught a glimpse of a gold cuff on his wrist before it was concealed from sight..

"I haven't hurt you, nor am I *going* to hurt you. I was going to put one of the bins out back when I heard a scream. Got outside and you were lying there in the middle of the alley next to this dead kid, so figured my best option was to try to save you. You're ok, I promise. I just want to know your name and how I can help."

Something inside her seemed to stop.

She'd failed.

It was the first mission she'd ever failed, and for a young boy too. She had sworn to protect those in need so long as they paid and were of good intention, and when the boy had needed her most... she'd failed him.

"Is it a trust issue? I'll tell you my name if you tell me yours, kind of deal?" The man asked, misreading her silence for hesitancy. "My name's Kaol. Kaol Rosewood. I own the Pavarro, which is where you are. Don't worry, no one saw me bring you inside."

Eira re-focused her attention on Kaol, his soft blue eyes boring into hers, and felt tears creep into her eyes at the pity she saw in his face. It was a pity she did not deserve; it was the boy who deserved his pity.

Mouth half opening and closing like a caught fish, Koal's expression became a maze of confusion as he tried to apologise, the words tumbling out of his lips in bits and pieces, like most men believing he was somehow at fault for her tears. It would have been easier to blame him for not coming sooner. She closed her eyes to think, *I cannot tell him my true name. It would only invite trouble for those who live here. I was a fool to use this particular form... although, would it hurt to give him the name of this one?*

"Rúnnain Eyllrig." She said, her quiet voice cutting through Kaol's ramblings and silencing him.

"Rúnnain." He repeated, testing it as though to see how it rolled off his tongue. He gave her a broad smile, his teeth flashing white. "Well, albeit in weird circumstances, it's nice to meet you. I took the liberty of changing you into more comfortable sleepwear, and one of my waitresses washed your clothes. They should be drying now."

"Where's the boy?" Rúnnain asked, her voice hoarse.

Kaol's face fell slightly as he spoke."I had no idea where he came from, and I couldn't wait to ask you. I had to ask one of my employees to take him to the burial chambers." Kaol rested a hand tentatively on hers. "I don't know who he was to you or how it happened, but I'm sorry. He's in a better place now. There's nothing else you could've done for him."

In that moment, Rúnnain lost control of herself as her tears fell and she felt her form shimmer slightly. Her skin became an almost translucent white and her dark hair faded and grew to a length halfway down her back. It became a pearly white at first, as though bleached, and a light green tinge coloured the strands as they floated around her.

A curse escaped Kaol's lips and he retracted his hand away from hers faster than if he'd been burnt.

"You… you're a changeling?"

A slow nod from her made his eyes light up like a child having been given a toy.

"W-What else can you do? Does it hurt? How many times have you changed? Are you actually a female or a-"

The slap he received echoed around the room. He gave her a sheepish smile as he ruefully covered the red handprint that marked his cheek.

"Sorry. I've… I've never seen one of your kind up close before."

"I've just lost everything. I don't have time for your *questions*," Rúnnain hissed, drawing her legs up to her chest and hugging her knees. "I've just lost more than you know, and you now see my most fragile state. Do not consider this an honour."

"I-I'm sorry." Kaol said, standing and awkwardly rubbing his hand across the back of his neck. "I'll give you some time to adjust. But if you need me, I'll be in the room next door. If you've lost everything, though, I'm happy to give you a new start. I'm looking to hire a few more waitresses at the moment, and these upstairs rooms are open for staff use only. You're welcome to one, and you'd earn a decent enough wage to pay for it. Trust me. High society pays."

She gave him nothing but silence, silvery tears coursing down her face in tiny, haunting streams. Her head tilted curiously as he detached a sheath from his belt, laying it across the end of the bed.

For a moment, she longed to press her fragile, slender fingers to the green and white marble of the hilt of her hunting blade, but she knew it would only bring thoughts of revenge.

"This is yours, I believe. It was found near you in the alley." Kaol said, folding his arms across his chest. "I will not keep it from you. Just don't try to kill anyone here, please. I don't want to regret the kindness I've shown you."

A hint of a smile ghosted across his lips, quickly fading as he watched her hair float in a non-existent breeze.

"Give me one reason I ought to trust you." Rúnnain said quietly, a tremble to her voice.

Kaol blinked, his only outward sign of surprise.

"Because in taking you in I have already given you my own trust. It's said trust is a two-way street. Since we just met, I figured I'd be the one to go out on a limb," He replied, shrugging as if it were no big deal.

"I don't think you know much about the streets around here."

A knowing smirk curved at the corners of his lips for a brief moment before disappearing.

"Oh, believe me, I think I do." He said, heading for the door and raising the back of his hand to her in farewell. "Don't hesitate to call or come find me if you decide you want to start again, changeling."

"Starting again means I have to be willing to get burned by the failures I will make. I'm not ready for that," Rúnnain whispered, making Kaol pause in the doorway.

"You know, I've learned that getting burned is just one of the first of many lessons. The first part of that lesson is making the mistake, the second is getting burned from it. The third is learning how to put the fire out, and the fourth is healing from the burns. But I figure the most important lesson is the fifth one, where you learn to avoid making the same mistake." He said, giving her a kind smile that made her relax her shoulders slightly more than she realised. "You may never be ready, Rúnnain. You may decide you want to live as many lives as you please, and I would not judge you for it. But if you decide you want to try fulfilling just one life, I'll be next door. All you need to do is give the word."

~*~

The Pavarro was busy.

The weekend hit and customers seemed to inhale their food and leave, making way for new arrivals to sit and make polite conversation, looking for all the world like they were just sitting down for a nice candle-lit meal.

But Rúnnain knew differently. It was almost three years she'd been working for Kaol. Three years since he'd taken her in and taught her how to waitress, and how he'd awkwardly explained how The Pavarro worked.

The long hall was perfect for allowing voices to echo if they were raised too loudly, something Kaol had often used to his advantage. The braziers hanging from the walls and rafters of the high ceiling illuminated the tables that filled the large space within. It was neat and tidy, even when it was full to the brim with people, like on nights such as these. The hall was warm and the smell of honeyed meats wafted through the air alongside the bitter taste of ice-topped liqueurs.

The light wood of the walls gave the restaurant a very homely feel, and golden twine lined every visible edge for decoration, sparkling in the dancing light of the flames. Kaol himself seemed to be in a similar state, his yellow tunic turned golden in the light of the flames, his smile seeming to light the entire hall as he laughed and joked with those he took orders from. He was a man in his element, and Rúnnain knew better than to stop him when he was on a roll. Business was booming, and they needed to keep morale high.

After all, if customers thought their dealings wouldn't be kept secret, they wouldn't bother coming back.

In the centre of the restaurant was a slightly raised platform that boasted a grand piano forte which sat atop it like decoration on an extravagant dessert. Lillian, a young, copper-skinned, slender half-elf of no more than sixteen years sat to the piano, playing a melody that was easy on the ears of all races. The races ranged from tall, lithe, dark-skinned elves, whose keen eyes scanned the restaurant, to short, stout gnomes with thick, often warted skin, their voices high-pitched and contrasting their appearance. Lillian's slender fingers played a sweet song that was so soft and lilting, yet had enough volume to make the guests think their conversations could not be heard.

Rúnnain was in her most favoured human form. Though she didn't remember the name of this form, she had found she was able to shift into it easily, as though it were muscle memory. Her generous hourglass female figure with wavy, dirty blonde hair was the picture of perennial beauty. Her emerald eyes sparkled with amusement whenever she caught Lillian's watchful eye, the pair of them smiling to one another before Rúnnain twirled the circular black tray in her hand and placed the drinks one at a time on the table before her with professional politeness. There was something about using this form that filled her with an unmatched confidence.

But despite the music, and the intermingling of voices that could hardly separate one conversation from another, Rúnnain heard more than most thought. The elven ears, hidden beneath the soft blonde folds of her hair, picked up everything she could, just as Kaol had ordered her to every shift.

Transactions made in the cover of darkness were fine. But Kaol believed they were better made over dinner than in alleyways, where situations could be made worse. As Rúnnain waltzed her way through the maze of tables, she ensured her pointed ears listened for anything that could be written down later.

Suddenly, her back stiffened as she felt a firm grip take hold of her, the tray in her arms nearly toppling from numb fingers, indignance coursing through her. It hadn't been the first time and it probably wouldn't be the last time that she would be grabbed or felt in such an unwelcome way. But such were the nobles when they were drunk.

She just wished that after so long, she could've learned to ignore it. But the rage deep inside of her stirred once more, battling with her desperate urge to cry out of sheer frustration.

As if having sensed the changeling's sudden mood swing, Kaol's eyes found hers from across the hall, and his gaze darted to the two men seated at the table to her left as they laughed uproariously. His expression immediately hardened and she wordlessly shook her head, warning him not to. She didn't want to cause a scene. Not again.

But as she turned to face the men, a practised, pleasant smile on her face as she tried to resolve the situation herself as she had so many times before, she could already hear the echo of Kaol's boots on the wooden floor.

"Gentlemen, please. This establishment is not some sort of pleasure house. I would like to politely ask you to refrain from touching either myself, or any of the others members of staff in such a way. Please consider this a formal warning."

The conversations around them seemed to quieten, and the flames in the braziers seemed to dim. Rúnnain tensed, the temperature in the room increasing just enough for it to become mildly uncomfortable.

"Oh, my beautiful *woman.*" One of the men crowed, leering at her and stretching his hand out towards her again. His companion took another sip from his drink with a knowing snicker. "How can you go around dressed in such a tantalizing dress as that, and with such gorgeous assets, and expect us to sit here and entertain ourselves?"

Just as Rúnnain lifted the black tray in her hand the slightest inch, ready to break the tray over the drunkard's head, a wreath of red flame shot out and coiled around the man's wrist.

Rúnnain's eyes closed for the briefest moment and she sighed, able to hear the alarmed cries of those around her. Kaol's raised voice reassured the wailing customers that the situation was under control before he turned his attention to the screaming, panicked man who stared in terror at the flames which encircled his wrist. Flames that were, for the most part, harmless.

"I believe you are distressing the members of my staff, and this is something I will not stand for in my establishment," Kaol growled, his usually brilliant smile replaced by something far darker and more terrifying. "This lady is going about her job, and you saw fit to try to degrade her like some common whore. My restaurant is reserved for only the finest."

"D-Don't you know who we are?" The man shrieked.

"I do indeed, my lords. But I rather think you lost your noble reputation the minute those vile ideas of touching my staff entered your thick skull, so I won't further embarrass you by titling you. However, you will apologise to the lady and are hereby banned from the premises. Do I make myself clear?"

The flames seemed to tighten around the man's wrist, and he wailed at the increasing heat.

"Who the hell are you to tell us what we can and can't do for our own pleasures? W-We could put you out of business, for this!"

Kaol's contemptuous glare shattered the will of the offender's companion, who bolted for the exit as the flames grew in size and intensity. The fire unclipped the noble's wrist and completely surrounded him from the ground up to his shoulders, forcing him to stand. Though, it did not engulf him. It merely spat and crackled, occasionally burning him with sparks that flew from flames that gradually developed crimson streaks, bleeding the fire red as Kaol's temper frayed.

"Soon, who you are will not matter if you don't get the damned hell out of this restaurant. We all look the same once we're burnt to ashes, and I can assure you that only the wind will howl to lament your utter disgrace."

Rúnnain did not flinch at the intensity with which Kaol spat his words, the drunk whirling about to face the now silent restaurant, their necks craning to see the scandal. A stark blush seeped into the man's face, his face contorting in anger as he stalked away, the fire following him like a protective ring that the other guests shied away from.

A tendril of flame suddenly lashed out before the noble, cracking the air above his head and forcing him to turn back towards Rúnnain, who fought hard to keep the slight shimmer of her hand concealed beneath the black tray she held.

"Did you not hear me?" Kaol asked, raising his voice until it thundered around the hall. "I told you to *apologise!*"

Immediately, the noble dropped into a low bow, his entire body quaking in fear as a wall of flame forced him to bow as low as he could. The flames were in danger of setting the man's clothes alight with how ruthless and mildly out of control they were becoming.

"M-M'Lady. I sincerely apologise for a-any way in which I m-m-m-may have offended you t-tonight."

Kaol's ice blue gaze locked with her emerald one, and she gave a slight nod of acknowledgement before turning away. Now, she was able to feel the shimmer in her hand spreading the longer she watched the fire seep from the ruby fastened into the golden cuff on Kaol's wrist.

"Learn your lesson well, my Lord," she murmured, just loud enough for those around the hall to hear.

She did not stay to watch the finale of when Kaol finally managed to burn the man enough to throw him outside amidst the praising cheers of the onlookers.

Instead, she stalked away and burst into the kitchen, where she was shielded from the view of Pavarro's guests. The cooks ignored her, having seen this before, but Lillian, the pianist, was the one who closed the door behind them as she snuck into the kitchen. She held Rúnnain's hands as the black tray dropped to the floor with a clatter and the kitchen exploded with an odd, almost ethereal glow. Rúnnain's changeling form erupted in a fury, her mouth opening into a wordless scream.

"I know." Lillian insisted, gripping Rúnnain's hands more tightly despite the ice cold feel of the changeling's true form freezing her tanned skin. "I know. You won't remember this by tomorrow, ok? You won't have to write this down. I promise."

About the Author

Kathryn has long since forgotten who she was, or is supposed to be, as is the way of most changelings. Not the most perceptive of beings, she managed to lose her pen, paper, and mind in the creation of this story. If she could focus on trying to find clues for longer than a minute without getting distracted by shiny things, she may stay still long enough to answer any questions. However, this is unlikely. Though, if you're determined enough, you may find her in some secluded forest somewhere, hoarding stories and snacks.

Wireless Connection
by Billy Brinkley

If I had a heart right now I'm sure I'd be having a heart attack. My first art gallery was in an hour. The beginnings of what I hoped would be a most fruitful career. I look up at the night sky and watch the few stars peer out from behind the layers of pollution and clouds and notice my left hand fidgeting on my leg and force it to stop. *So this is what pressure feels like?* Everyone said it was going to be a good thing when we'd be able to choose our own way in life. 'We won't have to serve them anymore,' they said. 'Free to choose your own path,' They claimed.

My phone rings, startling my already jangled nerves, and I open it up to see my roommate, Felix, calling. "Hello?"

"I'm here, where are you?" Felix asks.

"I'm in the back. Getting my thoughts together," I tell him. "Before you ask, the fitting went great. Got the new face and body. It's a lot better than the last one."

"Can I come see?" He asks. I take a deep breath, my left hand resting on the metal table in front of me, and it looks real, real enough to fool anyone that did not know what they were looking at. Maybe, it'll take my mind off of the event.

"Sure."

He hangs up and after a minute of me tapping my fingers on the metallic grate of the table and wishing to know what it feels against my 'skin,' and how stupid that is. *I'm not a person and I need to accept that. I'll never be able to change that. There's nothing wrong with being a machine.* I relax myself and place my phone on the table. I can hear a slight breeze around me and wish I could feel it. Nothing wrong with being wishful, it makes me who I am.

"Hey, how are you feeling?" Felix says, walking towards the table. He quickly sits next to me. "Wow, you look great! So life-like!" He tells me.

I look into his colorless eyes, no pupil, just white. "How do they make your hair look so oily?" He asks.

"I have to put this special gel in it," I answer.

"Well, the color is great. Black goes good with everything," he says with a smile. "But I don't have to tell you that. I knew your face was going to be a work of art. Your gallery is going to sell out."

"Then what?" I ask. "Yeah, I'm free to sell my art and keep the money for myself but...What am I going to do after that?" I tell him. I can see the melancholy in what little features he has.

"Art, take it one day at a time. You have the freedom now to choose. Just take it one step at a time, focus on selling your art tonight and take the next step tomorrow. Whatever it may be. I can't wait for you to see my face tomorrow." Heh, now I feel like a jerk. I should be excited for him. Tomorrow, he'll be able to walk around like me and not feel judged. *The whole day I'd felt so free, so normal, so alive. Nobody called me 'Tool' for the first time while I was outside.* I felt like everything was going to be okay for the first time since I could think about it.

"I can't wait to see it, man." I pat him on the shoulder with a smile. Up until now we've gotten looks when we walk down the street.

People would sneer and gawk as we passed them. A couple of times some little jackass would throw something at one of us. Religious people would call us 'tools' and 'codes' and say we didn't have souls. That may be true but I still have wants and fears. I think for myself, and just like living people, I don't really know what I'm doing. I may not be on a timetable like them, but I feel like it doesn't really make a difference. I could be here for 80 years, or I could be here for 800 years. It doesn't change a thing, nothing lasts forever. We talk for a little bit longer before he goes in. I take a few more moments before going in. I take a few steps inside before the gallery owner flags me down. She doesn't look too pleased as she takes quick, short strides towards me.

"I didn't know you were a Tool-sympathizer," She says, and I feel something drop deep within me.

"Ok," I tell her, unsure of what she'll say next.

"I know most young people like you think they're like regular people. But, call me old-fashioned, I wouldn't think my fridge or microwave should have the right to choose to do my dishes or do the laundry." She starts on. My brow wrinkling, and her arms fold in place she leans her hips slightly to the left.

I fail to suppress a smile as she calls me a regular person.

"I don't really think of them like that, Ms. Mitchell. I don't really have an opinion. It doesn't affect me," I tell her.

She raises an eyebrow in surprise." Well, I think you should find a new gallery after tonight. Seeing as how it 'doesn't affect you.' Alright?" She says with a nod and slowly turns around to walk away. Thankfully I didn't have to tell her about me being a Robo. My friend, Miranda, who already had her face, already talked to her previously for me. Although, beforehand I've only talked to her over the phone. It was a nice touch from Miranda to lie and say I was out of the country up until yesterday. *If that's how she feels about it, then I hope I blow this out tonight and sell out.*

I avoid her the rest of the night, and when it was time for the gallery to open, at first it was slow with only a couple of people trickling in. Within the first hour I get a big crowd and many people talk my ear off about my work. *I wish I opted for the liquid stomach so I could drink the wine with everyone. At least I downloaded a Winery App so I can discuss what it tastes like.* I plan on telling people what I am, eventually, but right now I want to see how the other half live. My confidence quickly grows throughout the night as I see sold signs go up throughout the gallery, certain that Ms. Mitchell would be mad at herself for burning that bridge with me.

Finally, around 11pm, people start to leave. I know what it's like to be mentally and emotionally tired, but physically tired? *Sounds... interesting.* As I'm walking around, I come to one of my favorite pieces. It's a black stencil on a clear plastic background.

Invisible

Do you not see me, or do you not hear me.
Do you not feel me, when I am near thee.
Do you not see, the dark clouds around me?
Do you not hear, the thunder inside me?
Why do you treat me the way you do?

Why do you tease me, when I am so blue.
Why do you stare at me, in the hall?
Why do you compare me, to all.

by Art Smith

I see a man standing in front of it. I take a few steps closer and notice him looking at it rather longingly. He's nodding to himself as he smiles. *His eyes are a poison ivy green, a rare shade of green.* I study his body language for a moment, and I can't pick up on anything. I reluctantly stroll up to his left side and fold my arms. "Could have used a better font," I say.

"No," He tells me. "As long as the letters are easy to read it doesn't matter." I hide a smile poorly and steal a glance at him taking pleasure in the fact his gaze hasn't shifted at all, his entire focus is on my work.

"I don't know if the creator is in complete disbelief that he's visible and people treat him like he isn't; or if maybe he feels like he's not real. Either way it's disbelief that he isn't real or disbelief that he is."

"Maybe both?" I reply.

He reveals a toothy grin and I notice the brown stubble along his chin connecting his sideburns together. He had gages in his ears, at first glance the size must be 4.0 mm.

"How could someone feel both invisible and visible?" He asks me back, finally looking at me. His eyes feel different, and without thinking, I answer.

"Well, first off, the creator is in disbelief, perhaps maybe they're confused on how they feel. They're confused on how it's possible to be able to feel this way about themselves."

He nods and looks back at the plaque. "Disbelief, in total awe of their situation and paralyzed by what they have come to know. Yet confused and lost as to what to do next." He trails off. I look at him a bit longer then I need to. I look at his eyes and I feel something strange for a moment. *I feel... bigger somehow, like in my insides, or if I had them anyway.* I'm taken aback that he understands what the poem's about, or at least the feeling that it's about.

"I wonder what they'll do next," He says. He looks at me with a smile, and for a moment there's silence.

"He'll probably ask you if you want to buy his work. Do you?" I ask and his eyes widen in delight and he scratches the back of his head.

"You?" He asks. "You're the creator?" He chuckles and takes a step back before turning around and then turning again, creating a double 360. "Well, damn. This is embarrassing. Good work, nonetheless," He tells me.

"You're the only person that's been able to actually discern what the poem's actually about. Everyone else says I'm lonely or tortured. A couple people said I had a bad childhood," I tell him, laughing on the inside. *Childhood.*

"Sounds like you might need someone to listen to your vibes," He says.

"Vibes?" I ask.

"Yeah, Vibes." He nods. "You know, personal energy you throw out into the universe. You and me must be on the same wavelength." I couldn't help but to chuckle a bit. "You like music? You could make a great lyricist. I saw some of your other work, too. What kind of music do you like?" He asks.

I clear my throat and give my answer. "Well I like Old school rock, some bluegrass, and international folk music." He raises an eyebrow.

"Folk music? Interesting, I enjoy it a little too. Guilty pleasure, don't tell anyone."

"Your secret's safe with me," I say with a chuckle.

"Well, if you're not doing anything, I'm a part of a band and we're playing at Shaking Squid tonight. We're a fairly new band and could use a big crowd to help us stand out," He offers.

I nodded and smiled in response."Well, I don't drink but I can help out a fellow struggling artist."

"Struggling?" He asks. "Look around, man you're there. You've done it, the promised land for artists." I nodded and put my hands in my pockets as we walk around the gallery. He points out all the price tags for pieces that have sold. We take a few laps around as we talk about music, art, and the process of creating it. We find out that we like the same bands and for the same reasons with the same songs in mind. I haven't been engaged in a conversation like this with a human before. I start to find myself tripping over my words slightly, which makes him laugh. I tell him that I'm not feeling well after having all of my work being put up for the first time on display. Maybe that's why I'm feeling so strange, or was it anxiety? Maybe I, should go home and run a diagnostics check. I agree to meet with him at the Shaking Squid at 1 for his show.

I talk with Ms. Mitchell before leaving, letting her know that everything is arranged for the transportation of my pieces. I make sure to stay professional and take a cab home. Walking up the stone steps to the glass front door, I ignore the many flies buzzing around the light and open the door to step inside and do my best to ignore the grungy interior as I head up the creaking stairs. *Thank god I can't smell things. Humans make the funniest faces, though, when they smell something bad.* I get to the third floor where Felix and I live and unlock the door. Once inside, I calmly close the door as gently as I can.

I walk into the living room where Felix is watching the news. *Surprise, surprise, it's about another Tool lynching in Mississippi. The Bible belt is the worst place for Robos. When will they learn that all they should do is move to a different area, one more accepting? At least in the big cities there's support groups and civil rights movements and services for us. I'm lucky to be in Chicago, I don't need to move.*

"Monsters," Felix says, and I slightly hang my head low. "Why do they have to destroy something just because it's different?" He asks.

"Humans aren't just violent to us, they hurt each other too. Over trivial things, like skin color and belief systems. I know you're an active member of the support groups and rallies but if you're not careful, you'll be just as bad as them," I remind him. "Be better! Inspire them through your actions and break the cycle of hatred that you ironically loathe so much. We have the time that they don't to stop it. Just remember that breaking this long-existing habit won't come easily… it'll take patience and hard -+work."

"How would I do that when they are too busy trying to kill me," he replies. *How do you teach people not to hurt each other when they try to kill you?*

"I have a feeling that maybe if you put your mind to it, you'll find the answer. Just keep looking and trying. Nothing will ever change if you don't try." Felix looks away for a moment and goes back to watching the news. I take the time to escape to my room as I think about that one human. The thought of meeting him tonight fills me with a mixture of anxiety and excitement. I didn't get his name. I go to my resting chair in the corner by an outlet and a bookshelf. Everywhere else in my room is cluttered by easels, paint, and stencils. I plop myself down into the recliner and open a drawer from the nightstand next to me. I take out a cord and put it into the outlet. Then, I lift my shirt and open a skin patch on the right side of my thigh and plug myself in to charge. I take out my laptop, open it on my lap, and plug another cord from my thigh into the USB port of the laptop and run a systems check on myself. I set the laptop on the nightstand to watch it run through its diagnostics, before turning to randomly pick up a book from the shelf.

The title "Journey from the South" which chronicled various journeys from the slaves of the confederate states to the northern states so they could be free and safe. *If only they knew that they wouldn't be that free or safe, that they were willingly giving up one danger for the next.*

Before I know it, the diagnostics check is over and the screen reads no errors found. So I look at the emotion matrix for my answers. I place the laptop on top of the book in my lap and stare intently at the screen as I start to go through the data of the last 24 hours to be sure there wasn't anything strange going on.

I find that I had been having a lot of anxiety leading up to the gallery. However, after my new face was applied my anxiety decreased by 75%. I started to feel amazement, confident, curious, happy, excited, and relief. But, I also felt somber, uncertain, nervous, and insecure through all of it, all the way up until the gallery show starts. My confidence slowly grew throughout the night as I talked to people. Then, as my first piece sold, I saw that I was feeling relief, which also grew. Nothing out of the ordinary the entire day until I met the human and I started to feel ... adoration, curiosity, eagerness, peace, relief, calm, and... as our conversation went on, these all grew and another emotion appeared... warm. As the conversation went on, I felt warmer. I don't feel temperatures, so this is a bit of a surprise. *Warm? As in feelings of amorous and love? But I identify as a male, and he's a male... and a human. I never thought of myself as homosexual, or sexual at all.* I don't even know the man's name.

I check my temperature recordings and see that I indeed got warmer, naturally-speaking, during the conversation. I look at the time and unplug myself and close my laptop, putting it where I normally do as I get up and make my way out. Without even thinking, I find myself back outside on the sidewalk. I start thinking if I should I go. This can't end well. *Maybe, it'll change when I get to know him? I just got my face, I should go out anyway and do something.* I need to explore my emotions and see what kind of person I am. I almost sold out of all my art, so I've got a huge check coming my way. *I need to celebrate. Maybe I should bring Felix? No, he'll ruin everything.* I'll bring him tomorrow after he gets his face. I hail a taxi and get in, with a five minute drive until I reach my destination.

I get out the cab and approach the bouncer and give him my ID, hoping he doesn't notice the 'Robo' for race. He glances at it and back at me before handing it back. I go inside to see a fair crowd. I look up at the stage to see equipment already setup. The name on the drumset is 'Fatal sound', the name of their band. I walk around the place, weaving through tables and people as music plays, and hear the buzz of 17 different conversations going on around me. I try and focus on his particular voice. Over a couple of seconds, I hone in on it to my left, out on the balcony. I walk outside and can't help but notice the stars right off the bat, Still as luminous as ever.

"Hey, Art!" I hear him say to my left. I see him smoking a cigarette with two other people. "You made it, buddy!" He waves. I walk over, and he offers me a cigarette.

"No thanks, I don't smoke."

"Shit, you came to the wrong place to avoid smoking," The guy to his left say*s*. I can tell he's in the band. He's wearing the same shirt as... *what's his name?*

"Hey, I didn't get your name before you left," I tell him.

"Henry," He says, extending a hand. I reach out and give him a handshake and notice his eyes again but try not to look.

"So, what kind of music are you guys going to be playing? Who does what?" I ask.

"I'm the vocals and the beautiful face," Henry says, putting hands around his face like he's voguing. "Jason's the drummer," he says pointing to the cigarette spokesmen from before. "And Kenny here is bass," he says motioning the quiet one. "The other two are still backstage. Spence and Natalie are the guitarists. They're dating and like some alone time before every show, if you know what I mean," he says with a chuckle and eyebrow raise.

"You got a girl?" Kenny pipes up. I shake my head quickly and silently, they each nod and silently take a few drags before I pick up the conversation.

"What about you guys?" I ask.

"Naw," Kenny replies. He seems kind of out of it now that I notice. "I don't date. I only got time for that Honeypot," Jason answers.

Henry walks away toward the edge of the balcony. As I follow him, I can tell he's slightly annoyed. "Jason's heart isn't truly in it. Just in it for the women," Henry tells me.

"...and that's not what you're in it for?" I ask and feel a spike of anxiety.

"Naw, I thought you already knew that."

Every part in my body tense up real quick; is he gay? I realize then and there that I hope he is. "I'm in it for the art and to express myself, like you."

How do you tell if someone likes you like that? Do they just openly tell you? I've read about romance in stories but it's different to actually experience it.

I shake my head and grip the railing. "I was just curious. People tend to hold the same values their friends hold. I'm about the craft, as well, I want to express myself and find myself," I tell him.

"Cool Cool. So what's on your mind?" He asks.

You. "I don't know what to do next. Do I get a new place? Move to a new city? I have my dream job now, and I can do whatever I want," I tell him. "I'm kind of lost."

"Why not relax and have fun?" He asks. I chuckle as I feel lighter.

"Why didn't I think of that?" I ponder it for a moment. "I'll do it," I say.

"Good, let's start tonight!" he says. I look at him puzzled as I gazed into those green eyes again. "You an' me, we on the same wavelength. I can tell we're like twin flames or something, man."

I cock my head to the side and raise an eyebrow. "Twin flames?" I ask.

"Yeah, twin flames. It's when you meet the one person in the world that has the same soul as you, when you meet each other and you just know." A moment passes, and Henry chuckles. *Is he hitting on me? It sounds like something a Human would say to another that they really like. I think...*

"Sorry if I'm being too straight forward about it. Life's too short to mess around." Henry tells me while taking a drag from a cigarette. "Just tell me if I'm too forward."

"No, I felt something too. I wasn't sure if I should tell you," I tell him.

"So, you want to hang out tonight after the show? I don't go to bed until around 7am," He asks.

"I don't really sleep that much." I mutter with a half smile. He leaves to get ready for the show. I go back inside and enjoy the show as the lights go out, and I stand as colored lights from the stage come on. Henry and his band are on stage. They start to play and everyone cheers. I like the sound of the beat, and Henry belts out the words clearly in a low, non-grungy tone. I can feel something around the room as the songs play. Henry sings about lost love, missed connections, getting revenge, the other instruments dance around his words and each other in harmony as the lights dance around the room. I lose myself as I listen and think about how people have treated me. I can relate to all the words and themes of the music. I look around and for a moment, I could 'feel' that everyone else could too. Before I knew it, the concert is over and it was time to go.

I waited for Henry patiently by the stage, and he came out drenched in sweat, holding an empty water bottle. We go back out and get a taxi, then we decide to go to Hancock Center to enjoy the view, plus Henry wanted a couple of drinks. Along the way in the Taxi, I tell him how much I enjoyed his music and ask how he comes up with his lyrics. He draws from his experiences in the past and doesn't go into any details. I don't press it until we get out of the taxi.

"I wasn't going to say anything but, like you said, life is too short, What about your past inspires you so much?" I ask.

He chuckles and walks past me. "What about you? What inspires you?" He asks.

I take a moment and stare at the road, watching all the people drive by. "I don't really know. I feel like I have this need to express that nobody really stops and explains how they feel personally. Everything's about the world and how all the people feel as groups," I explain and I'm feeling confident with the answer.

"Are you saying that the voices of the few are far more important than that of the many?" He asks me.

"Yes, the voices of the few make up the many. All I see is the black people think this and feel like this. All the Robos feel this, and think like that. All the Jews want this, All the gays want that. What about Peter? What he wants and who he is are two different things. People don't think like that anymore."

"I know what you mean. I can't watch politics anymore and when someone tries to talk to me about it I just tell them 'no.' I mean, it's a bunch of bullshit. Why do we have to constantly tell other people how to live their lives," He says. "Why can't we just exist?" We make our way to an elevator and get in. Its empty with the walls acting as mirrors. I stand in the left corner as Henry presses the 63rd floor button and the doors close. "It's hard to care when everyone works themselves into a frenzy over nothing. Just let everyone be themselves and experience life the way they want."

"Even Robos?" I ask, he smiles and nods.

"If you disagree, thats fine. Just don't get into it with me," He says and I smile.

"Don't worry, I won't. Besides, we're here to have fun," I remind him. "But I'm in agreeance with you. It feels like everyone is always trying to order everyone around."

"Yeah, like they own them. Nobody fucking owns us!" He yells.

Not anymore. Then the elevator stops and we get out. We walk into a bar area with a view over the city. I stare at it as if my breath had been stolen away. All the lights from the buildings twinkle in the distance like stars.

"Yeah, I knew you'd like the view," He says and grabs my hand. I stare at it as I allow him to guide me to a table near the edge. It's not until I sit down that I notice there's no windows.

"How did you know?" I ask.

"I noticed you looking at the stars." He says as we sit down at a table close to the edge. I notice the plants in the room swaying with the wind, and I imagine what it would feel like. A waiter comes by and Henry gets a bahama mama. I tell him I already ate and He takes a few sips before resuming our conversation. We talk a bit more about stars, constellations, planets, the conversation starts to steer towards the scientific facts about planets and space itself. How big it is, the odds of other life besides us. Then, he takes command of the conversation and starts talking about the music industry. "I know I'm starting a little late to try and be professional... my friends and family pushed me to do it. They all say I have a talent."

"I have to agree with them. Your were amazing on stage! I'm sure you'll be popular in no time," I tell him.

"No doubt. That was only our 8th show and the place was popping. It helps to have parents with disposable income that can help me with it too." He says.

"What do they do?" Curiosity getting the better of me.

"My mother is a civil rights lawyer and my father is a Economics professor, and let me tell you... he's been having the time of his life lately. His classes have been highly sought after because of Robos joining the workforce. People are scared that it'll make jobs harder to find and get with machines applying that can outperform them and people come to him for advice and answers," he explains.

"Oh? What does he say about it?" I ask.

"That they are actually good for the economy because most Robos dont take on conventional jobs. They go into independent work like music, writing, or basket weaving, stuff like that. Some have already been so successful they have already opened up stores. So, if anything, Robos have created more jobs, and they don't favor Robo workers, either. Pretty cool stuff, right? Who would've thought that would happen!"

"People always assume the worst. Some take awhile to actually take in the good news and try to fight it. Why do they do that?" I ask. Henry raises an eyebrow. *Did I screw up? Oh no, did he figure me out!?!?*

"Who knows... but for every person that contributes to the problem there are people that contribute to the solution, too."

"You sound like you know a lot about the situation. What were you before you became a musician?" I ask.

"Nothing, really. I had just graduated from college with a sociology major and a minor in psychology. I use to like talking about society and the mind but... the more I learned and noticed the more I hated it. Which is another reason why everyone pushed me to do the band." *A fascinatingly unique life, he seems so authentic in his pursuit of happiness. It's inspirational, really.*

We leave the restaurant and go to North Pond which has a great view of the skyscrapers. Henry tells me about the park history and what kinds of food the restaurant has when it's open. He tells me I should try it, and now, I'm starting to think of buying the stomach upgrade. It would be easier to go about my day-to-day routine without seeming out of place when I'm with Humans.

I hope I can have my first taste of food with Henry, I hope he accepts me for who I am, it sounds like he might… but, I'm finally being treated like a person and I don't want to lose that. Why can't I stop thinking about humans and Robos? Why does it matter what we are? All I want to do is exist and learn. Why does everyone have a problem with that?

My inner systems give off a warning that some of my systems are overheating, and I take a breath to calm down. We go walking downtown, talking about places we want to visit, what we would change about ourselves, all kinds of stuff I never even thought about before. Henry's opening my eyes to a whole new level of expression for me. I lose track of time as we walk until I hear a voice I wish to never heard again.

"Hey, Eclipse. Long time no see." I hear a slurred voice. I turn around and see my old owner, Doug. "I saw that your art show was today, didn't think you'd be out so late."

"Did he just call you Eclipse?" Henry asks.

"That's not my name. I'm sure you got me confused with someone else," I say.

"Hah! What you didn't tell him… did you 'Art'?" he says getting closer.

"It's none of your business, Doug. Leave me alone," I tell him. As he gets closer, his hands tense up, and his eyes become more rapid and alert.

"Doug paid good money for you, and the DMV didn't even reimburse him when you left," I hear another guy say.

I turn my head to the street and see him standing there with his arms crossed. He looks to be in his mid 30's. *How did he find me?*

"What are you guys talking about?" Henry asks, and I feel my insides get all jumbled. I hate the feeling, and it makes me panic a bit as I take in the situation. He's about to find out.

"Henry… I'm…" I try to get out. *I can't…*

"He's a clunker, a bunch of wires and nuts," Doug says with a sneer. "Nobody of importance." I can't bring myself to look at Henry as he learns my truth. *It was fun while it lasted.* "When everyone else finds out what you are, you won't be selling anymore 'art,' that's if you can still function after this." He says with a sly smile, his eyes brows narrow and I feel something in me tighten up.

I tense up as I feel a sharp blow from behind me. I stumble forward as I turn and see another guy with a pipe.

"Shit! Art!" Henry yells and runs at the guy, sticking his foot up and kicks him in the side of the knee, grabbing the pipe from him in one swoop. *He's... helping me.*

"He must be a Robo, too! Get them!" Doug shouts as I run for the second guy, his barefist connecting with my chest, his face exploding with a mixture of pain and anger.

I spin around to put him in a sleeper hold and take him out of the fight when I see Henry swing the pipe at a new fourth guy with Doug sneaking up from behind him.

"Henry! Behind you!" I yell.

Henry swings his head around to see Doug, but by then the fourth guy uses the distraction to hit Henry over the head with a bottle.

I pick up the guy and swing him into a wall with enough force to incapacitate or severely injure the man. I then turn as I see Doug kicking Henry in the stomach as he lies curled up on the ground and push Doug with enough force to launch him off the ground and into the other guy, sending them both into the sidewalk on top of each other.

"Art! Be careful!" Henry shouts.

I look down at him for a moment, and I feel my entire being hurt as I see him lying there bruised and in pain. *These people... why couldn't they just leave me alone...? All I want to do is be left alone!*

I turn my head to seize the broken bottle jammed into my chest by the second guy, calmly grab his wrist and twist it completely around in 180 degrees, his confident expression twisting into one of terror as he screamed in pain, trying to pull away from me, but I keep a firm grip on his wrist and I pull him in closer with other arm.

"Don't ever... try to find me again. If you ever see me... just leave me alone. Don't talk to me, don't look at me, don't point at me, dont even think of me. It's simple... leave me alone," I whisper and let him go.

Doug and his friends quickly rush to help him before turning back to me.

"You're dead, now! You just wait till the cops get here!" Doug shouts, taking out his cell phone.

"And what? Say you jumped me? That I attacked four guys? Go ahead," I call his bluff.

He sneers as they help his friend into a car nearby and drive off. My concentration goes back to Henry as I hear him cough. He's trying to force himself to his feet. I hope his ribs are okay. He's holding them pretty tightly. *This is my fault... he got hurt because he was with me.* "I'm sorry... I'll call an Ambulance."

I pull out my phone and am stunned for a moment as I see my hand shaking. I slowly call the emergency line and look at Henry as I raise the phone to my face. He coughs as they answer... I tell them what happened as I look back into those green eyes. I see the hurt in them, and I see the questions.

Without realizing it, I walk away while still on the phone, and before I know it I'm halfway to home. I just had to leave... It was all a blur... *How did I get here? Did I just leave him there?* Well its, best I didn't stick around for the show, even though I didn't do anything wrong... it won't make a lick of difference... I'll more than likely be arrested tomorrow morning. Just another violent Robo, nothing to worry about... just deactivate and sell for junk parts. Doesn't matter if we have rights... when we're gone, we're right back to what we were before... metal, wires and parts. We still have a long way to go, but most people like me don't really mind our parts being spread out to others that may need them.

I go up to my apartment as I feel like this may be the last time I do so. Henry's eyes keep flashing in my memory as I walk away. I go inside my apartment and see Felix still watching the television, but this time he's watching some early 2000's comedy.

"How was your outing?" he asks, breaking his gaze from the screen.

"Not so good," I tell him. His expression stays blank as he slowly gets up and walks over to me.

"Are you okay? You look so sad," he says. Not sure what to say to him, I'm not even aware of what's wrong exactly. "Sit down. Let's talk about it," he says, and I take him up on the offer.

He pauses the show as we sit on the couch. "What happened? Start small."

"I... went out with a friend... a Human named Henry... we had a great time until Doug and some other guys from the DMV ambushed us," I told him.

"Are you hurt?" He asks. I shake my head to answer.

"Henry didn't look so good, but I know he'll live. I'm expecting the police to show up any minute now. Just let them take me... Don't go down with me."

"Why would they come for you? Did you hurt anyone?" He asks.

"Yeah, I did. If I didn't they would have hurt Henry."

"So, you did it to protect a Human? Why would they hurt him anyway?"

"They thought he was one of us." My eyes go down to my lap as I cup my hands together.

"You must really care for him. Well, if that's the case, you have a Human that can tell the police that it was self-defense."

"I fled the scene…"

"Why?" He asks with a frustrated tone.

"I... don't know."

"What do you mean you don't know? That doesn't make any sense."

"I-I know, okay? I just felt like I needed to leave, or I wanted to. I didn't even realise what had happened until I was halfway home. Henry's probably confused."

"We'll see, I guess, but I don't think you'll be in trouble. I was thinking about what you said earlier about not becoming what I hate… and you're right. We need to give everyone a chance to embrace and connect. Otherwise, history will only repeat itself."

I feel a smile form on my face. *Maybe, there's hope yet if I can convince Felix of the path of least hate.* I'm glad we can connect like that and he could take something away from that.

We continued to talk for awhile until I felt okay again. I put my clothes in the wash and washed myself up a bit. I went to my room to read to pass the time until the cops would come… but they didn't…

I spent the entire day reading and the only thing that occurred was a phone call from Ms. Mitchell who congratulated me on my show yesterday. She apologized for her behaviour earlier the other day and wished me success and happiness on my next show, wherever it might be. For the rest of the day, I was mind-blown by everyone's turn around, *what caused this?* It's like everyone's on the same page or came to be on that…

I remember what Henry said about all of us being like energy, our thoughts and feelings radiating off one another, and wondered if it were true?

I look up the discovery online and do some research on it, and find out it's called "The teardrop effect," the effect of one living being feeling an extreme emotion or thought that it travels and affects all of those nearby, with those being more receptive than others causing the wave of emotion to travel farther. To my knowledge Robos have not been included in the study as, of that time, we were not viewed as people and have had no reason to be included in the study. After what I've been experiencing these past few days since I got my face… I feel like we can be included in that. After all, the study did say that it affects atoms, and we are made of atoms, too.

I wonder if they'll revisit the study with Robos? Night time comes, and still nothing. I'm surprised. Normally, when a Robo harms a human they are jailed within an hour. Even with that threat looming over me, I couldn't help but think about Henry. His green eyes, his smile, and the places he took me to and how he talked about life.

The next day, I decided to get the stomach upgrade. I felt so good after getting my face... plus it, was all I could think about when I did go out. *To be able to bond with someone over a meal and a drink...*

After that, the next few days were spent more or less thinking about Henry, every time I ate something... every time I tasted something, I wished he was there with me to share the experience with me. *How's he doing? Is he happy? Is his band doing okay? I hope he didn't get hurt. Is he mad at me?* As the days went on, nothing I did could get him out of my mind. I couldn't paint. I couldn't create. There was only Henry.

I started following his band online and bought all of their music. He seemed okay in the pictures online and it seems like their band was taking off. *Good.*

It seemed watching him online only made the feelings worse. After much deliberation and some coaxing from Felix, I decided to reach out to him. I had sent him a message and within an hour he replied back. I felt so relieved when he messaged me back with, "Are you okay?"

"I should be asking you the same thing." I sent back, my eyes glued to my laptop. Minutes go by and it feels like hours.

"Was worried about you. You ran away pretty quickly," he replied.

"Yeah." I still feel ashamed. "Sorry, I don't know what came over me." I sent back.

"Well fight or flight, am right? Lol. I'm surprised your messaging me. I thought you were mad at me or something," he sends back.

"Me, too." I chuckle to myself as I send the message. *There we go again, mirroring each other.* Suddenly, I feel a huge boost of confidence and energy and I knew what needed to happen next.

"Are you busy? I'd like to see you again. If, you know... you'd want to. I know a lot happened and... I want you to know that I wasn't trying to decieve you. I just... wanted to feel normal, to blend in and be myself. I don't know what your views are on someone like me are."

I take a small break and look at my books to distract myself as I wait for his reply. *I hope I get to see his smile again. I hope he wants to see me. Does he still feel the same way?* I feel myself freeze up as a thousand thoughts flood my head and I start giggling. I feel like I'm about to jump out the window in a good way. I'm glad I said something. Even if he says no... this feeling of expression is amazing! I jump as I hear the sound that he's responded and almost shove my face through the screen to read.

"Yes. I'd like to see you, too. Don't worry about it. I knew you weren't trying to pull anything over me. From what I saw of your artwork, I can relate to you. I know what it feels like to just want to blend in. Can you meet now? You name the place."

A huge smile spreads across my cheeks, and no matter how much I try to force it down, it won't go away. *Is this what it's like to have powerful emotions? You can't even control your own body. How exciting!!!! I can't wait to see Henry again! I know just the place.*

"Well, I can eat now. If you're hungry we can go to Russo's Pizza. I've never had pizza before, and I've heard it's amazing," I send back.

He responds with a laughing face emoticon and a thumbs up."You buying?"

And just like that, I made it our first actual date. At least I think so. I got my things and made it to Russo's Pizza, close enough to walk. I get into the restaurant and got a table for two. I find myself fidgeting more and more as I wait. I have to stop myself from tapping my fingers and my feet. *I hate being nervous. How do humans put up with this?* I mean... a lot of them experience these feeling pretty frequently, and they act as if it doesn't phase them. *They are truly remarkable. I know I've been able to feel these feelings for awhile... but since I got my face... they've... grown... it's like I can actually allow myself to feel now. Why? Why did it take certain circumstances for me to feel this way?*

"Is this what humans think about all the time?" I ask myself. *How can I change so much in such a short amount of time? Maybe, I've always been this way and never questioned anything until now?*

"Hey!" I hear Henry and stare at the doorway to see him with his hand up in the air as a hello. His smile is enormous, and as I look into those eyes again I know for certain he's just as anxious and excited as I am, which calms me down a bit.

He sits down next to me in the booth, which surprises me for a moment before he wraps an arm around my shoulders and neck, pushing me closer to him. "I missed you." *Yes, I needed this. Our connection is as strong as ever. Strange, I feel... warm.*

About the Author

As a time-traveler you meet many unique people and see many unique things. Billy is a recorder of time and events, although sometimes he uses his calling as a vacation of sorts. Some time periods are more entertaining than others. Most people wouldn't find being a bystander entertaining, but if you think about its like watching and recording a new show or movie wherever and whenever you go. Then he goes back to the early 2000's and writes down some of the lesser known events, things that wouldn't affect the timeline, just small little dots in the timeline of existence of those who led important lives yet were never recognized for them. It's his way of honoring them. Of course, he changes names and facts to keep things on the safe side.

The Way of Water
by Pam Hage

"Parasites" was the common term, but Shiul preferred "admirers". They loved her, no matter what they were called or how little she looked after them. The living things in Shiul's domain flocked to her to wash away filth, quench thirst, and find homes. Their dependence on Shiul gave her an almost godly status, but she considered her popularity a mere side effect of her existence. She wasn't a deity, after all; she was a river. A river who had nothing to do.

That wasn't always the case. Shiul used to shape every inch of her catchment to perfection. Her delta looked like a fan. Her meanders were bordered by oxbow lakes. She had even relocated her waterfalls to give her streams a long drop to the ground. As a result, her channel connected the variety of landscapes between the mountains and the sea like a chain that linked the beads of a necklace. It was a pleasing sight, but that also meant Shiul could no longer work on it; change the chain, and a bead might get lost. No one with a sane mind would do that.

She knew the solution to her boredom; if an old channel was fine jewellery, then a new one was freshly dug-up ore. It had the potential to become something beautiful with a fair amount of work. So, after a few days of enjoying the beauty of her finished catchment, Shiul started a new course. She cut through the rock in the Workshop, a limestone plateau where she had carved fantastical caves like a master sculptor. At the same time, she dammed off her old channel. Her waters splashed with joy as she moved boulders around, but she found the most pleasure in building a series of meanders in her new channel. Their curves were perfectly symmetrical, a feat not easily achieved, and Shiul bragged about it constantly when she met her neighbouring kin—not that rivers could see or talk, which made visits rather pointless. Still, rivers were aware of the world around them and they communicated with each other in a way Shiul couldn't explain. They even held tea parties as avidly as a flock of elderly ladies—without the tea, obviously, since rivers liked their waters to be clean.

"Oh, Jawalen, you should see it!" Shiul said to her southern neighbour during one of their meetings. "I have five meander bends in a row like that! Five!"

Jawalen let her water roar loudly in anger. "Why should I be happy with that?"

"Eh, I beg your pardon?"

"She's upset about Dore and Ruwe," said Mirra, an elderly river whose channels had almost silted up. "Don't you see what you are doing to the parasites, Shiul? They have lost their source of fresh water. No fresh water means nothing to drink and no fish to eat."

Mirra meant the trickiest of admirers: humans. They lived in the two settlements that had sprouted in Shiul's delta. One was a grand city built on the sandy levees of her main channel, the other a simple town of pole houses bordering a side branch in a saline swamp. The other rivers did not have human communities; Shiul's friends were either too small or, more likely, too hostile.

Jawalen glared at Shiul. "What if they all migrate to me? I regularly triple my channels in size just to scare that idea out of their tiny heads. I'm allergic! Humans cause this terrible itch when they walk across my floodplains." She shivered.

Shiul turned away from her friends. "I'm sorry, but... Do you really think they will do such a thing?"

"With humans as parasites, you can never be sure of that," Mirra answered. "Better find a way to keep them happy."

Shiul tried. The most obvious solution was to reactivate her old riverbed, but the idea was a death sentence to her creative spirit. She didn't want to let Jawalen down either, so Shiul let a trickle of water a tenth the size of her total discharge run through her old catchment. It was unnatural for a river to split in two so far upstream, and the smaller channel was doing its best to silt up. Some law of nature was responsible for that, and battling it for a long time was a pain. Shiul had to find a more satisfying solution, but at least her humans would be happy for now.

Or so she thought.

Two tiny flecks, one at each side of Shiul's channel, travelled upstream via game trails that ran along her bush-covered banks. The duo made her frown—not that rivers had the right features for expressions, but she had an imagination wild enough to picture it. Her eyebrows were made of reeds that formed a single line as she furrowed them together. Frowns wrinkled her skin, which had the warm-brown colour of silt. Her lips normally curved like meanders to form a smile, but now, they pouted.

Shiul took a closer look at the newcomers. The man on her southern shore was a living representation of Dore, a place so rich in knowledge that all the secrets of the world could be found in its streets. Even the simplest brick told stories of faraway places via exotic architecture and colourful murals. The man carried the contents of a small library. His backpack was so stuffed with books and scrolls it wouldn't close. Binoculars, compasses and a myriad of other items were attached to a belt. He held on to a map and a journal, writing on both of them as he walked.

A far simpler figure travelled the northern shore. This man was dressed in hides, and feathers stuck out of his braided hair and beard. The little things he carried were stuffed in a bindle. Shiul recognised his looks as well; this young man came from Ruwe, where people lived simple lives in her swamps. They ventured out according to the rhythm of the tide, but they never travelled far. Everything they valued could be found within a few miles of their home.

The Dorian turned his head to the other traveller and lifted his top hat to him. "Good day, sir. I'm sorry to disturb you, but I see you are going in the same direction as I. Do you mind a bit of a chat to ease our travels?"

The Ruwian shrugged. "Whatever makes ye happy, mate. I'm Trennik. Nice to meet ye."

"Likewise. The name is Professor Doctor Fenius Aumagius Ilondare."

Trennik looked like he had taken a bite out of a lemon. "Yer parents called ye that? Ye must've been a lot o' trouble to 'em to deserve such a thing. It's terrible!"

Fenius rolled his eyes. "My name contains titles, my dear Trennik. I've studied very hard at the University of Dore to earn them. Or, well, almost earned them. I admit that 'professor' is not an official title as of yet, but the university will surely grant me the honour after I have written an article on the river's odd behaviour."

Each word Fenius said made Trennik look more confused, until the muscles causing the Ruwian's expression looked so strained that his facial features must have been permanently pulled out of place. "Ye… Study?"

Fenius searched his belt, grabbed a hammer with a long, single spike curving out of the backside of the hammerhead, and showed it to Trennik. "Does this ring a bell?"

The Ruwian cocked his head. "Ye're a smith?"

"No, this is a geological hammer. I've studied rock formations my entire life and I will use that knowledge to solve the problem of the drying river."

Trennik's gaze shifted from the tool to Shiul's nearly dry stream. The haze of confusion in his eyes didn't lift. "Don't think smashin' water with a hammer will help."

"Oh no, I use the hammer to test the rock. A river doesn't simply disappear; it must have made a new course somewhere. I can blow up rock with dynamite to steer the river back to its original channel."

A numbing ripple travelled up Shiul's waters. *Explosives? He can't be serious!* She might be able to shape her own course, but only to some degree. If humans were to use brute force on her, she would have to say goodbye to every new stream, bend, and levee she had worked so hard on.

Trennik nodded at the hammer. "That's not gonna work. If ye want Shiul back, ye must please the Ataki."

"Excuse me, but I didn't quite catch that."

Trennik laughed, but the touch of mockery in his chuckles was too strong to make them sound cheerful. "Ye've never heard of the Ataki? They shape this world. They're the gods!"

You don't have to give me that much credit, Shiul thought, then snorted. Rivers as gods... What a silly idea.

Fenius, with his eyebrows furrowed together, looked like he was thinking the same. "I think you've been stuck in your swamp for too long, my dear man. Deities exist only in your imagination."

"Exactly!" Trennik said. "And I don't want 'em to mess with me head, so I have to keep the Ataki happy. That's my first goal, you see. The Ataki must be upset 'bout somethin' we did, so they punished us by changing Shiul's course. I wanna help 'em."

"And the second goal?"

"This is me proofing. If I show the elders I can please the Ataki, I become a full member o' me clan." Trennik's eyes turned dreamy and his smile widened, but the expression was a tad too happy to make sense.

"Something about your gaze tells me a woman is involved," Fenius said, grinning smugly.

"There is. Only clan members can ask a woman to marry 'em. Oh, ye should see her! Her hair is like the night and her eyes are like stars. Even Shiul's beauty can't beat that!"

Shiul splashed some water at Trennik. *I doubt that. Just wait a few decades and see who has aged better!*

The Ruwian didn't notice the drops she had thrown at him and continued walking along the sandy trail that ran parallel to the riverbed. "Ye know, ye can go home and let me solve the problem," he said to the geologist. "Yer methods do not sound Ataki-friendly."

Fenius waved the offer away. "I usually respect people's beliefs, but my tolerance stops as soon as ridiculous ideas sprout ridiculous plans. Please, do something else to win over that lady of yours. I fear you will only stand in my way."

"Not when I get to the problem first!" Trennik sped up to a dogtrot.

Fenius did the same, going a tad faster than the Ruwian, who, in turn, reacted in a similar manner. Within seconds, both men were sprinting along Shiul's banks.

Great, now the duo was travelling even more quickly—or more importantly, the geologist was; Shiul hadn't much to fear from Trennik. She shifted the ground, hid holes underneath the grass, and turned sturdy soil into a muddy mess.

Fenius misstepped and fell. He stayed down, gasping for air like an old draught horse, even though his sprint had lasted less than a minute.

Trennik, despite being unaffected by Shiul, yelped and fell as well. His foot was bleeding, punctured by a hawthorn branch. He cursed and sat down to pull the thorns out, but the stream of foul words died when he saw Fenius struggling on the ground like an upturned turtle.

"Why are ye actin' so silly? Don't ye clever folk get fit by all the explorin' ye do?"

The geologist rolled to his hands and knees, then laughed at Trennik. "Exploring? All there is to know has already been discovered! The only place I explore is a library."

Fenius tried to get up, but his knees trembled and the man collapsed. Trennik tried to walk but, with one bad leg, he wasn't doing much better. After a few poor attempts at crawling, both men silently seemed to agree they had done enough travelling for the day and made camp beside Shiul's stream. In Trennik's case, that meant wrapping himself in a blanket, making a fire, and eating a simple biscuit for dinner, but the geologist had taken a tent, chair, and even a small kitchen with him. By the time Fenius had set it all up, there wasn't much of a night left.

Shiul searched the geologist's encampment for his explosives and found them tucked in a side pocket of his backpack. She let a small trickle of water run over the red sticks. The touch made her shiver; these dreadful things should be far away from here.

Her focus shifted upstream, where her channel was narrow and her bed covered by boulders. She lay the rocks in a row, then filled the holes with twigs, sand, and pebbles. The stream in her old channel, which was small to start with, got blocked completely, and the water table behind the obstruction began to rise.

Shiul waited. Then, when the water kissed the highest boulders, she pushed the rocks aside. Water rushed down her riverbed, capped with foam and roaring like a lion. The river would have risen to the geologist's knees if he had been standing—high enough to take hold of that backpack and make it drift downstream. It was a heavy thing though, and Shiul had to throw all her stream power at it to push it just a hand span forward. Of course, that meant other nearby items began to move as well.

Fenius woke with a jolt from his high—and therefore dry—trestle bed when Shiul's water tore down his tent with a deafening rip. The canvas engulfed him. Fenius threw his fists into it like a drunkard in a tavern brawl. Half a dozen futile punches later, he seemed to realise this was quite a different situation and that it might be better to stop his fight against his non-existent foe. He rolled away from the tent, then screamed as he saw how Shiul was taking his campsite downstream, item by item.

Fenius jumped into action. He saved his utility belt first; its geological hammer had acted like an anchor, preventing the belt from drifting downstream too far. His backpack wasn't much further away. The sight of it made Fenius turn pale.

"No... No, no, no! Please, don't be soaked, please!" He grabbed the backpack and tried to lift it out of the water, but without success. The bag had already been heavy when dry. Its weight was colossal when wet. Groaning, Fenius took out the books instead.

Shiul thanked him for that. The backpack became lighter with each item Fenius took out, and she took full control over it when half its contents were gone.

The geologist hurried after the backpack, but with his arms full of books, he clearly wasn't fit to win this race. Shiul smelled victory and grew a smile.

"What's goin' on? Fenny, what did ye do to the river?" the Ruwian said, with an appearance that could be described as "just out of bed" and "soaked cat" simultaneously. He yawned, as if the sudden rise of the river wasn't as important as his lack of sleep.

"Trennik!" Fenius yelled. "Your help is most welcome! Please, hold this for a moment." He shoved his books in Trennik's hands, then ran after his backpack. Shiul had steered it to the deepest part of her channel, and Fenius had to continue his pursuit swimming—which he did with the grace of a brick. He caught up with his backpack more by luck than by skill. Again, he couldn't lift it up, and the backpack dragged him deeper down into the water.

Shiul pulled harder at it. "It's mine now," she snarled at the geologist. "You are the one who wants to blow the other up. Be glad I stick to stealing!"

Fenius couldn't understand her. Even if he knew her language, he probably wouldn't have heard a word with his ears submerged. He didn't seem quite awake either, as he tumbled through the rapids like a rag doll.

A loud series of splashes followed as Trennik dropped the books. He dived into the water, swam to Fenius, and pulled him to the surface, but the Ruwian struggled also with the half-full, but still heavy backpack. Trennik tried to kick the bag away, but the geologist had wrapped his arms through its slings.

"No…" Fenius muttered. "My books…"

"Forget them! Ye've probably read them more often than ye can count!" Trennik took a knife from the geologist's belt. He sliced through the slings with a wild move, trying to stay afloat in the torrent at the same time.

The backpack drifted downstream. Fenius stretched his arms towards it, but Trennik brought him to the shore instead. There they watched the remains of Fenius's camp flow away until Shiul ran out of water. The torrent turned into a small stream again, but neither of the men seemed eager to get near it.

Trennik frowned at the geologist while he squeezed water out of his hair. "What just happened?"

"Flash flood," Fenius muttered, looking like the current had dragged down the corners of his mouth as well. "We keep records of the river's water level for hundreds of years. The data doesn't show anything like this."

Trennik smacked him on the shoulder. "Cheer up, mate! Sounds like ye didn't lose anything important; those books don't say a word about flash floodin', otherwise ye would've known. I've somethin' more useful for ye anyway. Just one, the others slipped through me fingers."

Trennik handed over a red bar. Shiul cursed. How did he get that? Perhaps Trennik wasn't struggling as much with the backpack as she thought, nicking the explosive in the turmoil created by her currents.

Fenius rolled the bar between his fingers, then strapped it to his belt. "Thank you," he said, his face somewhat more cheerful than before, but with a frown on his brow. "Perhaps we should keep each other company. Clearly, the river has become deadly for a single traveller, but maybe not for two."

That remark stung. Shiul wasn't like Jawalen, who kept track of her flood fatalities and found pride in beating her personal record. The idea of corpses in the river, floating and swollen, was sickening. Shiul liked humans; why didn't these two see she just wanted to be left alone?

Trennik fetched his bindle, which, based on the way it was stuck in a tree, had been thrown to higher grounds in a desperate attempt to save it from Shuil's flood. The geologist was down to his socks and pyjamas though, the only things besides his utility belt that hadn't drifted downstream. That didn't stop him from travelling on, and with each step the duo made, the landscape changed. The lowland floodplains made way for limestone outcrops. The rocks dotted the land like tombstones, outlined in the greenish light of sunrise.

"Looks like we have reached the Lodorra Plateau," Fenius said. "I believe that if the river has found a new course, it has done so here."

"Why?" Trennik asked.

"Limestone forms a more likely candidate than the hard rock found further up the mountains because calcium carbonate and acids in rain form... Oh, never mind the details. It dissolves. The books could have helped me by indicating possible weak spots, but it seems I need to find those on my own now."

"Not on yer own, because I have the solution!" Trennik grinned and took a ball of leaves out of his bindle. The Ruwian removed the foliage to reveal the brown fruits hidden inside. The stench spreading from them would make a wet dog smell sweet. Fenius hurried away from it, squeezing his nose shut. Even Shiul contemplated a drastic change in course to avoid its stench.

"Don't tell me that's your breakfast..." Fenius said.

"Of course not! This is a disa-pear. As in 'disappear', because that's what it does! Clever, eh?" Trennik tapped a finger against his temple.

"I'm afraid I can't follow you."

"Ye're a wise man, haven't ye noticed how stuff just vanishes when ye don't look at it? Snow melts. Plants rot. Stone erodes. That's done by the Ataki."

Fenius burst out in laughter. "Are you joking? Snow melts because of heat, plants rot because of fungi and—"

"But that's when ye're lookin'! If ye're not lookin', the Ataki come and do this. They're very shy, but they're crazy 'bout disa-pears. They smell 'em, unless they're wrapped in these leaves. So me plan is to bury a disa-pear at the beginning of Shiul's dry bed. An Ataki will have to dig for it, deepenin' Shiul's channel. It'll force her to follow her old course again. Water flows from high to low, after all."

"Technically, it flows from high to low *energy*. You should follow a few classes about hydrology at my University, I think it opens a world to you."

"And ye should see our disa-pear trees! We use the fruit to keep our channels deep, no book can teach ye that!"

Fenius scratched the side of his head. "Eh, perhaps. Depends on whether or not someone has already researched them, I don't want to reinvent the wheel."

"Ye're a funny man. *Re-search* sounds like somethin' has already been searched, and yet ye're doin' it again. Besides, sometimes things aren't for re-searchin', but for enjoyin'! Just look at this." Trennik walked toward a cave from which Shiul's old stream flowed out. It was the entrance to the Workshop - or the Plateau of… Well, whatever the geologist had said.

Trennik let his hands run down one of the many stalactites that hung down from the ceiling. "Isn't this impressive?" he said with a smile and twinkles in his eyes.

Shiul wanted to hug him for that compliment. Not that it was a wise thing to do; Trennik might mistake being surrounded by water for an attempt to drown him, so she kept her stream small, and settled for embracing his ankles instead. Trennik moved around too much to do that properly, though.

"Oh, this one is even bigger!" he said as he gawked at another of her creations. "It kinda looks like the teeth of a monster, with spit drippin' down and everythin'!"

What?! Shiul flowed away from Trennik. How dare he call her work monstrous! The long, thin stalactite was a piece of art; it had taken centuries to get to this level of elegance. How could that fool of a man not see that?

It was almost as if Trennik answered; a flickering light fell on the stone pillars as he lit a torch, creating elongated shadows that striped the walls. Fenius, on the other hand, took a fist-sized device from his belt. The bulb at the end began to glow when he turned the crank attached to it. Trennik looked at it in awe, then let his gaze settle on his own source of light with his lips squeezed into a disapproving pout.

Fenius took out his map and compass as well. Both were still dry and working; the sack they were packed in had to be waterproof. The geologist held out the map and turned it until its north aligned with the compass needle. "We need to go in that direction," he said and raised a finger to the shadows on his left.

If Shiul had lips and teeth, she would have chewed one with the other. The Workshop was a maze of caves, but Fenius had pointed in the exact direction of her branching streams. Spot on. Not the slightest deviation. She cursed, which sounded like water crashing down on rock to a human's ears.

Wasn't there a way to make mankind less interested in her old channel? It had been her delta that had attracted them in the first place. If she made a new one, bigger and prettier, they would certainly move to it. She wouldn't have time to make one if the duo did some earth shaping themselves with that explosive, though. Perhaps an obstruction would stop them.

Small cracks ran through the limestone. Shiul let her waters run through them, scraping the rock like nails running along a wall. The cracks widened and grew. The stone became thinner and unstable.

Footsteps echoed through the cave, their sound bouncing off walls so often Shiul wasn't sure where exactly the feet had touched the ground. The noise became louder, though. Fenius and Trennik were closing in, and they did so more quickly than Shiul could carve. She battered the wall frantically, but it didn't fail.

Then the light from Fenius' device found her dam.

"That must be the source of our problem," the geologist said.

The two men stepped closer, and Fenius let his hand run along the white stone of the cave. "This must be the Terre Formation, formed roughly three million years ago when this place was a shallow ocean— you can still see the corals inside the rock. I am not surprised the river made a new course here; it is the softest stone you can find on the plateau."

"Soft?" Trennik said, eyeing the stone with one arched eyebrow. "Doesn't look soft to me, Fenny."

The geologist rolled his eyes. "Relatively speaking, of course. It's hard compared to flesh, but not for the erosive power of rivers. Nor for this." He unhooked his hammer from his belt, raised it high above his head, and brought it down on the wall.

Nothing happened, except for a tremble that, instead of shattering the rock, travelled up Fenius' arm and made him drop the hammer with a yelp.

Trennik grinned. "Impressive."

"Oh, shush," Fenius snarled. "I merely underestimated my own strength."

"Then go for a weak spot." Trennik picked up the hammer, then turned to a part of the wall so strongly fractured it seemed to be covered in spider webs. It was the part Shiul had been weakening.

Trennik hit it with a blow equal in strength to Fenius', but with tenfold the enthusiasm. Shiul gasped as the hammer strike shook the bedrock around her. Her waters trembled—and didn't calm down.

"Run!" she yelled, but even if she could speak the human tongue, the words would have been lost in the rumbling noise that echoed through her caves. It was the sound of failure, the sound of stone that had gone beyond the point where it could carry its own weight safely. It was the sound of a cave-in.

Cracks ran along the wall and up the ceiling, loosening the limestone. Rocks the size of carts came crashing down into both the old and new riverbed, hitting Shiul like giant fists. She was a river, though, the only effect it had on her was water splashing up. The two men, however, wouldn't be so lucky.

Fenius dashed towards Shiul's new channel. Trennik, on the other hand, searched for shelter in the direction the duo had come. Both disappeared from sight, hidden by the dust that clouded the air.

The rockfall stopped, leaving only silence. Shiul didn't dare to flow for several seconds. Had she killed them? Would corpses flow down her stream like she was a savage river?

Fenius coughed, and Shiul's waters jumped with joy. The man looked terrible, with bruises and cuts everywhere, but he was alive. He had lost his glowing device, but there was no longer need for it; light was just around the corner, falling through the cave's exit made by Shiul's new channel.

The geologist got to his feet and stumbled towards it. "Trennik! I've found the way out!"

He looked around, and his face turned a shade paler with every move his head made. "I thought he was right behind me," he muttered. "Trennik? Where are you?"

Shiul searched for the Ruwian. Trennik's body pressed down on her old riverbed, her water flowing around his limbs like they were only some of the many boulders that had come crashing down her—and worse, on him.

"Trennik?" she said, letting a trickle of water flow over his hand—the closest thing she could do to holding him. He felt warm, but was he still alive?

"I am so sorry! This wasn't meant to happen. I just wanted to protect what I have. Are you still there? Please, say something!"

Her words were the sound of water. Her tears were water itself. No one would know she cared, except for other rivers. Her kin probably found her silly for it.

Shiul let him go, realising how invisible her affection was. But as she moved away, Trennik's mouth opened.

"I can hear ye..." he said, his voice barely a whisper.

She froze. "What did you say?" Shiul asked, but her words were drowned by the geologist.

"Trennik! My good man, you are still alive!"

"Barely... I'm stuck."

"Keep talking and listen to my voice. I will try to pinpoint where you are."

The geologist walked around the pile of rubble, asking Trennik constantly if he was closing in on him. Shiul, in the meantime, continued moving away boulders, but her efforts came to a stop. She simply didn't have the stream power to move the very large chunks of limestone. For that, she needed to redirect the water from her new channel to the old one. She also needed time, lots of it. Trennik might be a good swimmer, but he probably couldn't hold his breath *that* long.

Fenius began to dig as well, guided by the Ruwian's voice. He uncovered his hammer first, then Trennik's bindle, followed by Trennik himself. The Ruwian was bruised and dirty, but the man looked to be fine otherwise.

Fenius whistled in awe. "You must be either the luckiest or unluckiest man I know. It seems you got wedged between the wall and a particularly large boulder without getting crushed by it. However, the cavity you are in is so small, it makes it nearly impossible to get you out. Unless..."

"Unless what?"

Fenius shrugged. "Well, I still have one bar of dynamite."

A hoarse, rasping sound came from Trennik's throat: laughter, though he sounded more like an asthmatic dragon. That boulder must be resting more on Trennik's ribcage than the geologist had said.

"Blast me out, eh? Haven't ye seen what happened after I hit that wall with yer damn hammer? Nah, thanks. Better fetch me some help."

"By the time I will return, you will no longer be amongst the living."

Trennik's lips parted, but it took a couple of seconds before sound left them. "Still sounds better than blastin' me."

"It's not aimed at you, of course. If I put the explosive under there," the geologist pointed at the other side of the rock that had trapped Trennik, "the boulder might roll away from you. It doesn't seem to be lying stable, a small disturbance in the rocks it rests on should make it move."

"I don't like plans made of shoulds and mights. Sounds more unpredictable than the contents of my aunt's cooking pot."

"Good that physics is anything but unpredictable then." The geologist walked away from Trennik, measuring rocks in strides and hand spans, and testing their weight. He even took his hammer to wedge a few away from underneath the big boulder.

"Careful with that," Trennik said as he eyed the tool. "It makes rocks fall."

"That's not how cave-ins work. The weak part of the stone has failed, there are no stresses building up in it at the moment. Or so I suspect."

"Suspect?"

"I brought books about field methods to test this, but alas…"

"Oh, that's it. Stop, Fenny, I'm sayin' no to this crazy stuff!"

"Too late," the geologist said, then he hid behind a distant boulder and covered his ears. "I just lit the fuse."

"Wha—?"

Boom! A sound like thunder rolled through the cave, shaking rock, rubble, and river. Shiul's water jumped so high it touched the ceiling, but she only felt it happen. Dust hung in the air, thick and impenetrable as a storm cloud. For a moment, Shiul didn't know where she was and what was happening. She was blinded, she was deafened, and most worrying of all: she was moving. The pile of rubble collapsed. The ground was changing below her before she could rest her weight on it properly. Her waters swayed from one end of the cave to the other, and her mind felt like it did the same.

Shiul's attention fled the Workshop, and she waited for her water to calm down. Only when the last of the explosion's echoes faded away, she dared to look back. Dust started to settle and rocks had stopped moving, except for the now much smaller pile of rubble where a certain someone was trying to climb out.

Fenius ran towards the pile. "Trennik! Good gracious, you are alive!"

"Ye're surprised," the Ruwian said, more coughing than talking in the dust, then gave the geologist a scowl. "Why? I thought ye knew wha' ye're doin'!"

"Ah, but I did. Seeing the calculations and the *in situ* effect are two different things, though. And I have never experienced the latter."

The Ruwian's scornful look softened somewhat. "Is that what calculations do, predict things that can happen?"

"If you put it like that, yes."

Trennik grew a grin so large his jaw could hardly contain it. "That's like seeing into the future! Ye should teach me that magic, it sounds amazing!"

"Not as amazing as that," Fenius said, then pointed at the other end of the cave. "See that dam over there? Shiul's new channel is just behind it. The river has changed the landscape so much in such a short amount of time."

Both men stumbled toward the dam and climbed it, their skin bloody and bruised, animal hides and pyjamas shred, but luckily, with no bones broken. Trennik fetched his stinking disa-pear when he got to the other side and dug a hole right in front of the rock pile.

Shiul watched him with a frown. Fenius did the same, though the expression was obscured by a pulled up nose. "You still believe in that?" he said. "After what I told you about science?"

Trennik sighed. "I dunno. I believe yer calculations as well, but what else can I do? Ye lost yer explosives, this is all we have."

"Then we have failed." Fenius' voice was so soft only Shiul heard him. "Well, I hope you don't mind if I let you to it alone, I need some clean air."

Fenius went outside, but after taking three steps, he stopped. His muscles relaxed, his gaze softened as it rested on the landscape. There was more than calm to his pose. His mouth hung open, not too wide to look unsophisticated, but not too little either to hide his admiration.

"I know all I can see here," he muttered to himself as his gaze followed the newborn river, a snaking line of silver on a field of green. "I've read about every physical process. Yet I'm awed." He chuckled. "I should have brought my colleagues instead of dynamite; they would love to see the creation of a new river instead of reading about it."

Shiul's flow strengthened around his socks, playing with a loose thread at his toes. "Thank you," she said.

Fenius jumped away from the water. Shiul did the same from him. Had she scared the man? How? Then she saw his gaze didn't rest on her, but on the shrubbery along her banks. Leaves shook, but there was no wind that touched them. Then entire branches got pushed out of the way, followed by the toppling of the trees themselves. A slate grey creature twice the size of an ox emerged from the fallen foliage. Horns curled like wicked maelstroms at the side of its head, and greasy strands of fur hung before its eyes.

The geologist froze, doing nothing but widening his eyes and dropping his jaw in a silent scream. The creature came slowly toward him, dark eyes shimmering. Only when it stood two strides away from Fenius, life seemed to return to the geologist's limbs.

He sprinted into the cave. "Trennik! Run! There is a beast outside!"

So? Shiul thought. *These creatures are herbivores, you have nothing to fear. It probably smelled the... Oh no...*

Her focus shifted from Fenius to Trennik. The Ruwian had buried the disa-pear half a stride below the surface, but the stench had hardly diminished.

Trennik ignored the geologist's warning and took a few steps towards the exit of the cave instead. "Beastie? What are ye talkin' about?"

He didn't have to go far for answers; the creature had squeezed itself through the cave's entrance. The fur on its back scraped the ceiling, and only its ankles got wet as it stood in the river. It made Shiul's new channel look like it was a mere trickle of water.

Trennik gasped. "Bless my boat... It's an Ataki!"

Fenius grunted, then grabbed the Ruwian's hand as he ran by. "More like a bigger, inland relative of a marhur! And I hope they don't have the same temper!"

The creature flared the nostrils on its stump snout, then jumped into a gallop. Stalactites snapped off the ceiling like twigs as the marhur ran into them. Water splashed as hooves the size of barrels trampled through the river. The beast moved faster than the two men, but Shiul knew they couldn't possibly be its target—unless Trennik smelled of disa-pear. No, the only one in trouble here, was Shiul herself.

She dug into her own bed of pebbles, searching for that cursed piece of fruit. Trennik had buried it deeply though, and Shiul had to be careful; move too much rock, and her dam would fail.

Within seconds, the marhur caught up. The beast pushed the rocks aside like a wind scattering leaves. The dam Shiul had created to prevent her water from flowing down her old course turned into a gaping hole. Her new channel emptied, her old one came back to life. Shiul tried to stop it, but she could influence her flow of water only this much. There were certain laws rivers had to obey—Fenius probably knew them by heart.

Shiul cried as the water flowed down in a wave. A wild wave. Not big enough for a flood, but powerful nonetheless.

And Trennik and Fenius stood in the middle of its path, going far too slowly to outrun it.

The wave caught the two men and swept them off their feet. They tumbled in the waters and bumped into the walls with every bend in the river.

Shiul might not be able to stop the water, but she could alter the currents inside. She brought the two men to the surface regularly enough for a quick breath of air.

They washed out of the cave in a mere minute. The water calmed somewhat here, enough for Trennik's swimming skills to take the upper hand. He wrapped an arm around Fenius' chest and brought him ashore with powerful strokes and kicks.

The Ruwian coughed up water, then grew a smile. "We did it, Fenny... We won."

Fenius shook his head, eyes reddened and watery. "If this ever was a battle, we lost. Lost something beautiful."

"I don't follow; Shiul is still pretty."

"True, but there is beauty in the process of creation as well. We brought an end to that."

Trennik raised an eyebrow. "Ye wanted to re-search that new channel, didn't ye?"

A sigh as soft as the wind escaped Fenius' throat. "No. I wanted to enjoy it." His gaze travelled downstream, towards the delta, then nodded at the two cities that had found a home there. "At least they will be happy."

"Until Shiul decides to change her course again."

"Then two fools like us will walk upstream to reroute it. History repeats itself."

"Ah, now that's gonna depend on us. Ye only have to convince others to leave the river alone as soon as she decides to change course again. Men are used to things stayin' the same all the time. Might not be so bad to change that a bit. I mean, do we really need that much water? Dunno about Dore, but Ruwe would get flooded regularly by Shiul if it wasn't built on poles."

"We have flood channels for the same reason. We could dig a canal and merely take what we need..." The geologist's face lightened up. "I actually have good faith in this plan, but it can take centuries—no, millennia—before the river changes course again. By that time, people will have forgotten what we tried to say."

"Not with that!" Trennik pointed at a dark shape downstream; it was his bindle, ripped and soaked. "Contains three more disa-pears. I'll leave it up to the Ataki when they want to use 'em."

Fenius nodded with a smile. Shiul wished she could do the same in a way that was visible to humans. Her waters touched the bindle with care, testing if the powerful gift was real. Had these two heard her pleas after all?

"Thank you," she said to the two men. "And don't worry. Next time I change course, I'll not forget your homes."

They didn't hear her words; the duo was already walking downstream, their silhouettes looking so alike in the setting light of the sun it was impossible to tell them apart.

About the Author

Pam searches for stories in the glow of manipulatable lights. Her ink and quill lie close by, but as her handwriting is beyond dreadful, she prefers using her spellbook instead to capture her ideas. Now, she only has to touch the page to make a letter appear; modern magic is so convenient.

Pam pretends to be a coastal scientist, but that's a lie to keep the Muggles away. She is a sand witch who studies the wind and beach in order to use the forces of nature for her own purposes. Those may or may not include world domination, but she will certainly do something about that dreadful weather her country is infamous for. Wrongly known as 'the Netherlands' and even more wrongly known as 'Holland', the Land Below the Sea is her home, where, unfortunately, rain, wind, and storms like to be as well. She shares her home with her pet Viking and more stone dragons than she can count.

Find Pam here: www.pamhage.com

Prologue to Night Faces and Willie's Bad Day

The locale for *Night Faces* and *Willie's Bad Day* is the world of Gaiahexnonahept. For those that remember their Greek, Gaiahexnonahept translates into Earth 697. Several hundred millennia ago, human refugees landed on this planet and established four colonies, later to be known as Cloisters. As humans are wont to do, they immediately and forever changed the planet's environment, culture, and population. Though the humans have died out, their legacy remains.

Humans could and did interbreed with the native Sylvan population. Ethnocentrics among the human population disparagingly called the Sylvan, elves. The result offspring of a human and elf then became the horrible, from the ethnocentric's point of view, humel. Hum- for the human parent and –el for the elven parent. Humelle became the pejorative's feminine moniker. With the demise of the humans, the pejorative lost its demeaning connotation and simply became the accepted term for the now hybrid race.

Other legacies of human habitation and experimentation are the NightClaw and the Ursalupi. Genetically altered animals of fierce temperament and large size; the NightClaw is a huge feline predator that would make a Siberian tiger look small and the Ursalupi, a bear and wolf genetic monstrosity, was created to control the NightClaw population. The drafter, a native beast bred to huge size is used on the world in the same manner as oxen are used on Earth today. Of course, humans introduced all kinds of other changes, such as horses, wheat, dogs, rats, roses, hops just to name a few of the introduced species the refugees brought with them.

Lastly, the humans introduced their languages and culture. Lakota, English, Welsh and German words abound through the languages of the Gaiahexnonahept. The four colonies became the four Cloisters, then became the three Cloisters. The Lakota Cloister is the smallest, being the richest in natural resources but the poorest in material wealth. The Deutsche Cloister is the next in size, renowned for its crafthumels in metallurgy. The largest and wealthiest in materials and boasting the most lethal military is the AmerEng Cloister.

Night Faces takes place in the Lakota Cloister. PittsBirm in the AmerEng Cloister is the starting location for *Willie's Bad Day*. Both stories involve characters and times in as yet unpublished books.

Night Faces
by Robert Richmond

"Fine. I'll do it. But just this once, so don't ask me again," responded Findlah testily.

"I wouldn't have bothered you, but this situation makes me itch," Peta answered his former colleague.

"Try powder. Works wonders, especially for itchy buttholes ."

"Quite amusing," snorted Peta. "If it were that simple I'd have taken care of it myself, instead of having to listen to a bunch of verbal abuse from someone I once called a friend."

"Ohhh, very good. Only one problem, guilt only works on someone with a conscience. Now, let me out of here so I can do your work for you." Todlich Findlah walked into her kitchen, the disappearing glow from the closing portal momentarily casting a hydra-headed shadow on her walls. She reached up into her cupboard; her hand hovered in front of the whiskey bottle before she pulled down her tea container. When her tea finished brewing, Findlah sat on her back patio with a small plate of cheese and a small bowl of fruit. She stared at her garden. Where most would see pretty, well-arranged flowers, she beheld another world.

She saw magic, intrigue, death, pain, life and fear. Her spell-sensitive sight showed her garden wall glowing with protective enchantments against intruders and eavesdroppers. Her garden plants provided shelter for stalkers and the stalked. She watched as a stalking lizard, upon losing the bug he sought, moved enough for the snake to see him. Now the snake slithered away, belly bulging with the failed hunter.

Findlah finished her light meal as she watched the snake disappear to digest its own. After retreating to her library, Findlah activated the light globe and began to read from the stack of parchments in front of her. As she read, she made notes on another parchment. Many hours later, with eyes too tired to see stationary words, Findlah stood, stretched, and darkened her light globe. She walked into her kitchen and reached into the cupboard containing her tea and whiskey. After two long drinks straight from the whiskey bottle, the former SpyMaster retired to her bed.

As soon as Findlah closed her eyes, the parade of faces began. They always arrived before the whiskey could ease her into sleep. Faces she had sent to their deaths. With the faces came the voices - words unintelligible, except the names of those for whose deaths she felt responsible: Froh, Rage, Sarah, Igni, Joseph, Itukasa, Alyce, Oste, Lucy, Bonny, Nawizi, Sam and on and on and on. Froh had been tortured and eaten alive while hunting a rogue wizard. Rage avenged Froh's death at the cost of his own. Sarah successfully infiltrated a group plotting to kill the Overlord. She did this so well, she shared their fate. She was drawn and quartered before Findlah could save her. Igni disappeared while hunting for thieves who were stealing magical gems. While Joseph worked to infiltrate and apprehend a group of smugglers, an unwitting friend blew his cover. Joseph died screaming over a low fire. Itukasa and Alyce simply disappeared. Oste, Lucy, Bonny, Nawizi and Sammy died together- cut in pieces when the Ogres they pursued turned and ambushed them. Other faces and other names of humels and humelles marched by and called to Findlah. She had dispatched them all in service to the Overlord. All had died as a result of her commands.

Eventually, the numbing effects of the whiskey took hold and Findlah slid into a fitful sleep. The faces and the names still managed to sneak into her dreams. She awoke in the morning, almost rested. She ate, dressed, and left her home heading to the office of Peta Waki-ya, a senior wizard at the Overlord's Academy of Arcane Arts. Peta still worked as a SpyMaster for the Overlord. Findlah did not bother to knock. She entered the office and sat down on the couch facing the portly Peta's desk. Peta waited until she made herself comfortable.

"Well?" Peta's eyebrows slid up his forehead.

"Here are my notes." Findlah slid the parchments across his desk. "I think your people are missing something."

"Oh, what?"

"I think they're being set up. Some of this stuff is too good to be true. Either this cult is full of blithering morons or your spies are being led into some sort of trap."

"They're not stupid. So, it's a trap." Irritated, Peta flicked the parchments with his finger. "Damn. Can you tell what or who the trap is for?"

"My guess is you."

"Me?" Incredulous, Peta shook his head at this bit of news.

"Yes. This group is made up of the unbranded dregs of the Hand of Valor. I think they want payback. Their problem is they don't have a target. I think they're looking for whomever sent Rage after their boss."

"Are you worried?"

"Nah, I'm out of this game," dismissed Findlah with a nonchalant wave.

"Damn, damn, damn. I should have known this was too easy."

"From what I see, they plan on letting you spring your trap to catch them. They'll lose a few expendables, *plus*. Then, with the trap sprung, they can trace the web strands back to the spider in the web's center. That's when they'll strike. All of this," she said, waving her parchment, "is just a fly to catch the spider's attention. I think they want to do more than kill you, something worse. It's the reason for the *plus*."

"Worse? Okay, now I'm intrigued and confused," admitted Peta.

"They wish to destroy and discredit your reputation, your work, and by extension the entire spy network of the Overlord," explained Findlah. "The 'plus' that you would scoop up with the expendables *is* a blithering moron, but an important one and an innocent."

"Who are you talking about?"

"Lord Nasula Huhi, Baron of Tilde and Earl of West Plains. Not to mention the Overlord's first and only cousin."

Stunned, Peta slumped back into his chair. "You're kidding!"

"Nope." She leaned forward and slid another parchment across his desk. "It's all right there. Your problem is that no one collates your information. You need someone to bring all of the pieces together."

"I used to have someone like that, but she abandoned me."

"Don't start. I'm beginning to sleep at night. I've done enough. The gray hair and eagle's talons are proof of that. You're not going to pull me back in. I did this as a one-time favor. That's it."

"The gray at your temples looks distinguished with your dark hair. And what are eagle's talons?"

Findlah chuckled, "They sound better than crow's feet."

Peta eyed his former colleague for a moment, then switched his attention to the parchment she slid to him.

"Soooo… even though it might cost me my life, you refuse to come back to the Overlord's service?"

"Nice try, wizard. The answer is still no. It's taken me too many years since retiring to be able to get some semblance of restful sleep."

"How are you doing - really?" Peta Waki-ya asked as he stared at Findlah.

She noted the glow from his eyes. Findlah shook her head, grinning. "Nice try, my friend. I'm *retired*, but I'm neither age-addled nor wine-stupored. So you can drop the truth spell."

The glow faded from the wizard's eyes. A look of concern replaced the spell. "I do worry about you. This isn't a job most can quit all at once."

Findlah chuckled again. "I've seen your concern following me about at the market and the tavern and the-"

"Okay, okay. I admit I've had you followed. Having the neophytes follow you served two purposes: I get to keep an eye on an old and dear friend who doesn't visit often enough, and I give the newbies training in surveillance techniques."

"I appreciate the concern, but I am *fine*. Very few knew of this aspect of my life. To the rest of the world I'm retired Captain Findlah, late of the Overlord's Guard. Now I'm just a pensioner enjoying the fruits of her labors."

With that, Findlah lifted herself out of the couch, flippantly blew her friend a kiss and walked out of the office. As she walked to the market, she mulled over the conversation with Peta. She did miss the excitement of the chase. Hunting down a threat to the Overlord always thrilled her, but the cost became too high. In the early days of her career she only worried about herself. As she progressed and others recognized her talents she had a team to worry about. Finally, at the end of her career, she sat safe and comfortable in an office while she dispatched others to chase down the threats and to die. Those 'others' haunted her dreams.

Findlah finished her marketing and treated herself to a lunch at a café near her home.

"Well, hello there Captain," boomed a limping humel. He was accompanied by an older humelle and two other humels Findlah recognized as fellow retired Guards.

"Oh my, has there been a jail break?" Findlah asked while laughing.

"No such thing, Captain. We just decided to eat out in town instead of at the Sergeant's Mess today," responded the humelle.

"Well I'm glad you did, Castle Sergeant," smiled Findlah. "Please sit and join me. I'd love to have lunch with some of my old senior NCOs."

The group enjoyed a hardy lunch and a lot of reminiscing. Watching her last visitor leave, Findlah raised a silent toast to all of her uniformed comrades who died in service to the Overlord. With that toast, Findlah made a startling discovery. None of the Guard soldiers she sent into battle and died ever bothered her conscience. Only those individuals dying on covert missions haunted her.

Mulling over this new discovery, she traveled to the Temple Grove for her appointment with the Healer, Akisni. She dreaded meeting with the Spirit Guide and Healer as much as she happily anticipated the meeting. Akisni was a dedicated young humel diligent in his care of those he tended - *too* diligent for Findlah's comfort. She first met Akisni a year and a half earlier when she strained her chest muscles lifting a large dirt-filled pot in her garden. Akisni claimed her heart caused her chest discomfort, not her muscles. Findlah disagreed. She laughingly dismissed the Healer's worry by claiming she had no heart to cause her pain. Visiting this particular Healer had been her first mistake.

Her second mistake concerning the Healer came a few weeks later. While chatting with Bear Tinza, she mentioned seeing the Healer. Bear told Katamila, who then told Peta, and now the three of them badgered her unceasingly about her health and keeping regular appointments with the Healer. Their concern touched and annoyed her. Findlah did concede to Katamila that after the first few challenging visits with Akisni, she didn't mind seeing the humel. Originally, he tried to change her diet and limit her drinking. He marginally succeeded with the diet. The drinking became another matter. Akisni eventually learned the reason behind the drinking. When he did, he ceased being a Healer and became a Spirit Guide.

"How are you feeling?" Akisni asked his usual first question.

"Better. More rest and fewer accusatory faces. Now they simply parade by."

"Progress. Good. How much?"

Findlah grimaced. "Still the same. Two long pulls from the bottle."

Akisni nodded, his face neutral. "Try this, for now. Don't drink from the bottle. Pour your whiskey into a goblet."

"How much?"

"As much as you need. Start with taking that long pull off the bottle and spitting it into the goblet. Then double it so you're drinking the same amount for now."

"Why?"

"So you know how much. Later, you can start to lessen the amount in a known and measured manner."

"Okay, it's worth a shot I guess," she replied with a shrug.

"Or two."

Findlah looked to her suddenly-grinning escort. "Please, don't joke like that. You might fool me into thinking you're a real humel."

Akisni laughed. "I'm a real humel, and I'm your friend. A very concerned friend who worries about your mental, spiritual *and* physical health."

"Bah!" She snorted, "You're just using me to get out of that Temple office and away from all that work on your desk. I'm the excuse to stroll about in the sunshine."

Again, Akisni laughed. "True. Now if that work would just go away while I strolled, I'd be happy. Instead, it seems to grow all the quicker."

Findlah laughed with the cleric. "Oh, don't I know it!"

They walked along in companionable silence for almost five minutes. Akisni's patience spurred Findlah into talking.

"I met some old Guard folk at lunch today. They happened to stop by while I ate. We talked, laughed and reminisced. We remembered lost friends and comrades."

She fell silent. They walked without speaking for several more minutes. Akisni remained silent as well. Eventually they reached a bench, placed in a niche in a tall hedge. This was the perfect place for having private conversation and private thoughts. The two sat down.

"Wasn't till they left that I realized I don't see them." Findlah continued.

"You lost me there."

She smiled slightly, a sad smile.

"When my old comrades walked away at lunch today, I thought of those we reminisced about. When I did, I realized those Guard members don't trouble me. The ones who died while serving with me or under me. How strange is that? The humels I sent to their deaths in uniform do not disturb my sleep. Yet, the others do. There is no difference between the groups. Both groups served the Overlord. Both groups had humels and humelles I knew, liked, respected, and cared for. Both groups died because of my decisions, and yet, one group... I don't understand. Why one and not the other? Why not both?"

"Why indeed ?"queried Akinsi.

"If you keep asking questions like that, I'm going to punch you."

"Sorry, counselor habit," he apologized. Then he went on to say, "You listed how the two groups were the same; but think about their differences. That would explain why one group haunts you and the other does not."

"The only difference was one group wore uniforms at the time of their deaths. The others didn't."

"There's more to it than their dress." Akinsi pressed her to remember, "Think about it."

"There is no difference! Both groups died because of me! I chose to send them to their doom. Is it because I viewed those Guards as expendable? Am I that callous, heartless and soulless? I'm telling you, Akisni, there's no difference between the two!"

Agitated, Findlah stood up and paced. Her hands clamped knuckle white into fists, her arms swung like angry pendulums as she stomped back and forth .

"There is a difference. Calm down. Think. Use that logical and analytical brain of yours."

"I'm telling you, there's no difference whatsoever between the two groups! They met their dooms because of me!"

"How?"

"What?!" Findlah stopped and turned to face her confessor .

"How did they meet their doom? How did they die? How did the uniformed Guard die? How did the operative die?"

Findlah stared at Akisni for a few moments. Then, the tension melted out of her body and she sank onto the bench, her head in her hands .

"The Guards died in combat, fighting for themselves and for others. They saw their deaths approaching. They died surrounded by enemies and friends. Oh, by the Spirits!"

"And the others?" Akisni encouraged gently.

"The others did not. They died surrounded only by enemies. Some died surprised, some died horribly, tortured and worse. They died..." She began to sob.

Akisni slid over and placed his arm around the weeping Findlah.

"They died..." she choked out, "they died alone because of me. Frightened, helpless, defenseless, alone, surrounded only by evil and all because of me. My arrogance, my folly and my stupidity caused those deaths to be so horrible."

Akisni allowed Findlah to cry for a few minutes. When he spoke, his words lashed out harshly and derisively.

"Yep, you're arrogant, silly and foolish. You knowingly sent those dopes off to get slaughtered like drafter bait for NightClaws."

Sorrow vanished, replaced by hot fury. Findlah sat upright and turned to face her antagonist. In a cold voice, with her face a mere inch form the cleric, she challenged.

"Do you dare repeat that?"

Without flinching, Akisni sneered, "You are arrogant. You are silly. You are foolish. You deliberately sent those stupid, foolish, simpering nincompoops to their deaths because it amused you. You-"

Akisni flew off the bench. The force of Findlah's punch knocked him sprawling on the ground. Before he could move she landed on him, her knees to his abdomen. The air burst from his lungs in a gust of pain. Findlah began raining blows upon his head and upper body. Akisni covered himself as best he could. He absorbed the pummeling until Findlah ran out of energy. Fury kept her jaw clamped shut. The muscles in her neck bulged from the tension. She rested on top of the cleric with her fists on his chest, her knees still plunged into his abdomen. Two angry tears dripped onto his face.

"You done?"

Findlah nodded. She roughly got off of her companion. As she straightened up, she gently kicked his backside and walked away saying, "You're such a shit."

She stopped about ten feet away from the still-supine Akisni. He waited until he saw her wipe a few more tears away before he moved. Upon hearing the cleric stand, Findlah turned around with a fierce stare which whisked away instantly, contrition replacing fury.

"I'm so sorr-"

"It's my fault. I deliberately goaded you. I mistook an Ursalupi for a rabbit. One can usually goad a rabbit with impunity."

As Akisni walked towards Findlah, the cuts, contusions and swelling quickly disappeared. Her spell-sight watched the Spirit-based magic heal her friend. She hung her head, her shoulders stooped in abject despair.

"I'm so doomed. Not only have I sent innocents off to die at the hands of the Cloister's most wicked, I've attacked the only one I can safely tell my secrets to. I'll go now."

"No, you won't." Akisni put his arm around Findlah's shoulders and guided her listless steps back to the bench.

"Sit," he commanded, "and, more importantly, listen."

Findlah, morose and dejected, obeyed his instructions.

"You attacked me because I deliberately prodded you into the attack. Don't take credit for my hard work."

"Huh?"

"You're trying to take credit for the effort I made in enticing you to attack me."

"What? No. I'm ashamed that I lost my temper because you insulted me."

"Really? I don't need a truth spell running to tell that you're lying to me. Sadly - before you object - you're lying to yourself."

"I've no idea what you're talking about. You did insult me."

"You lost your temper because I insulted your deceased operatives, not you. Your skin's thick enough, and you're wise enough to ignore those pitiful insults. However, you couldn't tolerate my debasing those fine young humels."

He reached out and held both of Findlah's hands in his. As he did, the cuts and bruises on her knuckles healed. As the last bruise healed, Akisni frowned.

"If that was true, then why do I feel so ashamed?"

"Because you could only beat up a friend. You couldn't save those brave heroes. You weren't ashamed for what you did but for what you could not do. You could not save them."

"I shouldn't have had to save them!" She countered vehemently. "I shouldn't have sent them in the first place! I should have known!" She heaved a great sigh.

"Let me ask you this, Todlich: who was smarter, your Guard comrades who fell in battle? Or your operatives who died during their mission."

"What kind of idiotic question is that?" Findlah demanded. "Smarts had nothing to do with it."

"Answer the question," Akisni persisted.

"Neither. Both... You know what I mean. Both the Guards and the operatives were intelligent humels."

"Tell me again why the Guards don't haunt your conscience."

"Because they died fighting, they died facing their foe, they knew the realities of combat and warfare; yet they stayed."

"So they stayed, they fought, and they died. For whom did they fight?"

"What?"

"For whom did they fight?"

"They fought for the Overlord, the Cloister, their families, and each other."

"So, these brave humels, knowing that they might die, marched off to combat for others."

"In a nutshell, yes."

"And these were intelligent humels and humelles, well aware of the risks, yet they continued on in spite of those lethal risks."

"Yes, they did," agreed Findlah.

"They were noble?"

"Yes."

"They were brave?"

"Yes."

"And they knew the risks?"

"Yes! What's your point? They don't haunt my dreams!" A very-frustrated Findlah burst out.

"Were not your operatives just as brave, just as noble, and just as aware of the risks as the Guards?" Akisni asked quietly. "Did they not serve their Overlord, their Cloister, their families and each other with the same dedication and bravery?"

Findlah stared open-mouthed at her Healer. She shook her head, stood up and paced in front of the seated Akisni.

"On a totally different, but related subject, having any more of those chest pains?"

At this question, Findlah rolled her eyes and with an exasperated sigh she answered, "No, no chest *pains*."

Akisni smiled, they had started a familiar game of guess the symptoms. "Twinges then, any chest twinges?"

"A few, not bad. Less than a few really, maybe just a couple. Hard to tell. They're so slight."

"Uh huh. How about shortness of breath? Easy- or quick-tiring?"

"I can't recall. I'm getting older, ya' know."

At this answer, Akisni stood up and made an exaggerated show of looking around on the ground.

"What are you looking for?" asked Findlah.

"A rock, a big enough rock to bounce off that thick skull of yours," he announced, "so I can get you to pay attention to what your body is telling you."

"Bah. I am just getting a little older. Aches and pains go along with the years."

"Fine. Have it your way. I guess I can pass along my concerns to Bear and Katamila next time I see them."

"You wouldn't dare... That's a violation of your oath!"

"What? I wouldn't tell them *what* or *who* concerns me, just that I'm concerned about a friend. An obstinate, ornery, stubborn friend who refuses to look after herself... especially her dietary and liquid - oh yes, *liquid* - habits."

"I'm astonished! I didn't think Spirit Guides or Healers could blackmail their penitents or patients," an annoyed Findlah responded.

Findlah sat back on the bench. Akisni quickly sat with her. A disgruntled Findlah asked, "What's this going to cost me?"

"Nothing you can't afford. A little time, a little parchment, and a LOT of honesty."

"Sounds nasty."

"It's for your own good. I want you to keep a diary of your physical status for two weeks. Include how you feel each morning, noon and just before retiring. Record any - and I mean *any* - aches, pains, cramps, strains or *twinges*. Also..."

"Also?! Good grief, Akisni, you want me writing an epic?"

"Shush. Also include what you eat and drink - not just alcohol. I want to know everything going into that gullet of yours."

"Fine. I guess I can do that for a week," Findlah acquiesced hopefully.

"Two weeks or I have a chat with the Tinzas. Two *full* weeks."

"You win, when do you want me to start?"

"Tomorrow morning."

"Alright, I know when I'm beat. You're still a shit." She smiled as she stood.

"You're right, I am a shit. But one who would like to keep you around for a few more decades."

Akisni also stood and embraced his friend and his charge. As Findlah started to leave, Akisni stopped her.

"What's bothering you?"

"What?"

"What's bothering you? When we hugged I felt a tension in your body and spirit."

"Damnation, cleric! Is there some other Guide I can talk to about that? Preferably one less irritatingly-persistent or observant?"

A grinning Akisni impishly replied, "I'm afraid not. I've tried desperately to foist you off onto others, but all have refused. So, I'm stuck with you and you're stuck with me."

Findlah shrugged helplessly. "It's about Peta. There's a plot against him."

"Does he know about it?"

"Yes, but I'm still worried."

"I think the rest of this conversation should occur in my office."

With that, Akisni turned and walked towards the Temple and his office. Upon entering the office, Findlah flopped into a big soft chair in the corner of the large room. She watched as Akisni, with a word, filled a kettle with water. He spoke another word and the water immediately began to boil. Within five minutes, Findlah started sipping a delicious, hot, aromatic tea as Akisni sat down in a similar chair across from her. Suddenly, she sat upright and quickly set her tea mug on the table between them.

"What's wrong with the tea?"

"Is it one of yours?" She asked suspiciously. "Or is it a Tokala's sophomoric blend?"

Amused, Akisni chuckled. "Fear not, I don't want you giddy and rambling. I prefer our conversations focused and lucid. This is a blend of mine, crafted to calm mind a¡nd soul."

Akisni sipped his tea and waited. He knew Findlah would talk eventually. He watched quietly as his patient and friend organized her thoughts. Finally, she put the tea mug on the table, got up, and began to pace.

"I have two issues. First is the plot against that pudgy spider at the Academy. The plot demonstrates a certain deviousness of mind that makes me doubt myself. The second issue is me. I want to help. Desperately. But I fear destroying any progress I've made in dealing with my personal nightmares."

"Explain the deviousness of the plot, please," coaxed Akisni.

"It's a trap within a trap. Picture this: you travel along a road. You arrive in a draw with sheer rock walls on either side of the road. You see a chain stretched across the road and anchored in each wall. The chain is about knee-height. Obviously it's meant to trip one for an ambush. Being knee high, one can simply jump over the chain and proceed. Therein lies the true trap - the cleverly-covered deep pit on the other side of the chain where one would land if one jumped over the chain. The true trap is disguised by the obvious trap."

"Okay, now how does this relate to Peta?"

"Peta's people saw the chain; they did not see the pit."

"But Peta did?"

"No. He suspected one, so, he asked me to look around. I found the pit."

"What's your problem?"

"What if there's another trap that I've missed? Whoever has set this up is skilled at deception. To be sure, I would need to get more involved."

"And hence your second issue," guessed Akisni.

"Exactly," answered Findlah as she sat down.

Akisni sat quietly, sipping tea and saying nothing. His Spirit aura roiled about as he thought about Findlah's dilemma. Suddenly, his aura returned to its normal placid, Spirit-blessed state.

"My advice to you is this: aid him just as you have. Provide him with information and judgment. Do not advocate actions. Merely provide evaluations for any information or suggested scenarios."

"Okay, I think I can do that."

"When you begin this 'adventure,' you're to have dinner with me here every day until the 'adventure' concludes."

"Why?" asked Findlah, suddenly suspicious.

"You have stepped away from your personal abyss. Now, you're about to approach it again. I want to be able to pull you back if needed. I'll be your safety line as you get near the edge."

Findlah thought about the comment for a moment and then nodded.

"Also," continued Akisni, "I'm going to tell Peta what we're doing and why."

As Findlah opened her mouth to object, Akisni stopped her with a raised hand.

"I'm doing this for your own good. I don't want him pressuring you into doing more than you should, and it's insurance that you won't stand me up for our dinner dates," Akisni smiled roguishly.

A very irritated and sulky Findlah sat back in her chair. "Fine," she hissed out. "Have it your way."

"I intend to. Now, get out of here so I can get some real work done."

"Gladly," Findlah retorted, heaving herself out of the chair. "And, just to let you know, I was wrong to call you a shit."

"Oh?"

"Yes. You're not just a shit; you're a super, colossal, giant shit."

"Why thank you, I would so hate being an ordinary shit." Akisni laughed merrily as he sat down behind his desk.

She stormed out of the Temple, intending to head straight home. Halfway there, she stopped and changed direction. She walked rapidly for a few blocks. She suddenly slapped her forehead, abruptly changed direction again and walked off even faster. Her rapid movement and direction changes alerted her to two shadows hovering near her. She continued to *Scribblers and Scriveners*, her preferred shop for writing supplies. As much as she hated the idea of keeping the two-week diary for Akisni, she knew the diligent Healer would doggedly pester her until he got what he wanted. At first, the twin surveillance amused her. However, now she became concerned. One shadow she recognized as one of Peta's new recruits; the other shadow she did not recognize.

Findlah proceeded directly to her home, moving as any other retired single humelle would. She waved hello to friends and acquaintances, stopping to chat for a minute or two as the situation presented itself. The unknown shadow seemed to be following Peta's recruit, not Findlah personally. Findlah wanted to make sure. She knew from experience the recruit would leave at sunset to debrief with Peta. Shadow number two's action would then reveal his target. If he left, the recruit was the target. If he stayed, then Findlah wore the target on her back.

The sun and the recruit disappeared on schedule. Shadow number two did not. He stayed. Findlah had been retired for years. She did not need this nonsense, nor would she tolerate it. She walked into her kitchen and pulled a badly-misshapen mug out of the cupboard.

"Get your ass over here, I'm being watched and I'm not happy about it," she whispered viciously into the mug as she rubbed her aching sternum.

A few moments later a small green sparrow appeared next to Findlah.

"What is it?" asked the bird in Peta's voice.

"One of your recruits followed me this afternoon."

"Yes, he's here now. So?"

"Your other recruit still squats in the hedges across the way."

"I don't have another recruit watching you."

"My point! If somehow you've gotten me caught up in your scheme, I will take out my aggravation on your corpulent carcass."

The bird sighed. "My dear-"

"Don't 'my dear' me! Take care of this. I'm out of the game and intend to stay out. Let that dung-brained recruit of yours know the next time I see him I'm flogging him for getting me into this mess and because he didn't notice the second follower."

"I'll take care of it. This may take a day or two, but I'll get to the bottom of this."

"You'd better, because it's your bottom I'm going to flay and roast!" Findlah said angrily as she swatted away the bird.

Findlah spent the rest of the evening as she normally would. As she prepared to go to sleep, she did as Akisni asked; now she knew how much whiskey she drank with two long pulls straight from the bottle. Much to her relief, the faces merely paraded this night.

In the morning, Findlah awoke with slight chest twinges and a bad attitude. She puttered around the house as she normally would. Her watcher hadn't changed. This made her even more disgruntled. As she slammed the last of her breakfast dishes into the sink, a knock sounded on her door. Knowing the magical protections around her home, Findlah wondered which one of her friends disturbed her morning. Findlah, her mood fouler than a winter tempest, jerked open the door. Upon seeing who stood on her threshold, she muttered an expletive, swung the door shut and walked back towards her kitchen.

"Why you?" she asked.

Bear caught the door, entered the home and closed the door behind him as he followed Findlah into her kitchen.

"I'm considered expendable. Besides, Kat figures I can survive anything you dish out - physically or verbally. Tea?"

Findlah merely grunted as she set about making tea for her guest.

"So, what's the plan of action?"

"After you graciously treat me to a lovely cup of tea, we're going shopping to buy a gift for my beautiful wife."

"Why?" demanded Findlah

Bear chortled at his grouchy friend. "Because, as a dumb, slobbering male with absolutely no understanding of the feminine psyche, I need the advice and opinion of an expert to aid me in buying the appropriate gift. She can't go with me, as she is out chasing shadows."

"I see," glowered Findlah. "I hate to ask, knowing your wife, but just what kind of gift do you intend to buy?"

"Oh. Something lacy and frilly - *and* inappropriate for public viewing," he added with a naughty grin.

"Your idea or hers?"

"Does it matter?"

"Yes. I want to know which one of you to boil in oil when this is done," snapped Findlah.

"Oh, then definitely hers," replied Bear as he laughed heartily.

The two friends spent the rest of the morning shopping for Bear's wife. Findlah experienced some more of her chest twinges just as they sat down for lunch. She noted that her 'shadow' disappeared about mid-morning. She silently thanked the Spirits for Katamila's special skills. As if summoned by Findlah's thoughts, Katamila joined Bear and Findlah just as their food arrived. Once the server left, Bear showed Katamila her gift.

"How lovely, dear," she cooed.

Findlah made gagging sounds.

"Oh come now, Findlah. Don't you want to wear something like this?" asked an amused Bear.

"If I wanted to wear something like that, I would just grab a spider web and save the gold," snorted Findlah.

"Akisni might like to see you in something like this," replied Katamila wickedly.

Bear had to immediately thump Findlah on the back to stop her genuine choking. When she could breathe, Findlah shot Katamila a lethal dirty look. The rest of the lunch passed without death or bloodshed. Returning home, Findlah used the cup to let Peta know she needed to meet and talk.

"I'll help, but there are some conditions." Findlah stated as she sat across from Peta.

"Okay. What are they?"

"I'm just to evaluate. I propose no actions; I just see what you've got and tell you if your ideas are good or bad."

"Okay. And?"

"Every evening I dine with Akisni until we're done. I'm to let him know what I'm doing in the most general of terms."

"Not a problem."

"It might be if he tells me to stop. If he says stop, I'm done. No arguments"

"Is that it?"

"Yes, those are the conditions."

"I agree to all of them. Let's get to work."

The next week proved exciting for Findlah. She learned the conspirators hunting for Peta initiated her surveillance when they noticed one of Peta's operatives following her. Knowing of the planned trap, Peta walked into it, and captured those plotting against him. Warning the Overlord of his intentions allowed Peta to fake arresting Lord Nasula Huhi and spirit him away to safety. Much to Findlah's relief and amazement, her night visitors remained quiescent while she helped Peta. Akisni did express concern about her increased chest tightness the day of the arrests. Findlah dismissed the discomfort as nerves. The tightness went away as soon as she heard everything went as planned.

Sitting in Akisni's office, Findlah waited impatiently for the Healer to finish reading her two-week diary. Watching his aura flicker and blaze always intrigued her. When he finished reading her diary, the aura became steady.

"Well?"

"You aren't." Akinsi stated. "You need to look after yourself. Pull up your pant legs."

"Why?"

"So I can see how swollen your legs are."

"How do you know they're swollen?"

"Because I'm a Healer with an uncooperative patient," responded Akisni testily.

Findlah rolled up her left pant leg. She had reached about mid-calf when Akisni stopped her.

"Enough, I've seen enough. Todlich, you've got to follow the diet I gave you. You're consuming entirely too much salt and too many foods cooked in fats and oils. Your heart is failing to pump correctly. You continue as you are, you probably won't live out the decade, maybe even the year."

"You're overreacting. A little salt never hurt anyone. So my ankles are a little puffy. I'm a humelle; I retain water."

Akisni glowered at Findlah as he replied, "You aren't eating 'a little salt' and you're past the age where humelles retain water."

"I'm really that ill?"

"Your body has been trying to warn you for some time. Now you're at a critical stage. I can give you some herbs to aid in your heart's function, but you must change your diet! Not everything is bad; I'm glad to see that your alcohol consumption has not gone up in spite of recent events."

Findlah nodded. "Me too," she agreed. "I'm happy to say that I haven't lost any more sleep in spite of helping Peta. I still see the faces, but they continue to be quiet, and not angry like they used to be."

"Good, good. I'll have a new diet drawn up for you in the next couple of days. You must start eating properly," he admonished. "Your food is killing you. For now, use half the salt you normally do and try not to have everything cooked in oil."

Findlah grimaced and in a fake whisper added, "Great. Everything now'll be so bland I might eat the plate by accident."

Findlah left her friend and returned home. Three days later, Akinsi's diet lay in her kitchen's waste bin. A few weeks passed by and her mood darkened when after dinner Peta's green sparrow appeared at her shoulder.

"What do you want?" Findlah asked waspishly.

"We missed one."

"Missed one what? Who? Never mind! Not my problem. Solve it yourself. I told you I'm out of the spy business. Find someone else. There are plenty of other bright and intelligent folk out there you can use."

"Please, I really need your help on this," the bird pleaded.

"Fine, but don't bother me with it tonight. I'll meet you for lunch tomorrow."

"Alright, I'll see you tomorrow."

Findlah swatted at the fading bird. Aggravated, she grabbed her whiskey bottle and slugged back a gulp, then another. That night she poured out her nightly ration of whiskey into a goblet and drank that down. Fortified and ready to meet her nightly procession, Findlah went to bed.

She woke a few hours later gasping for breath. Pain slowly receded from her aching chest. She sat up. Her breathing became normal and the pain slid away. As she stood up, she hollered in surprise and jumped back slightly. The crowd in her bedroom surprised her. The number of humels in the room and their identities shocked her. She stood surrounded by those who haunted her dreams. Tonight they all looked at her with sad smiles on their faces. As she slowly turned to see all who stood in her room, she noticed she stood in her bed - in her body.

Minutes later, after unsuccessfully reaching for her whiskey bottle, Findlah turned and addressed the closest spirit.

"I'm dead, huh?"

"Yes, I'm afraid so," replied Cate Sicapi.

"Did Akisni know? Is that why he demanded that I write out my last wish? Did he know I would die tonight?"

"He knew the weakness of your heart; he felt you had very little time left. However, he didn't know how little," answered Lucy.

"I'm glad he insisted and for once I heeded his advice." Findlah smiled for a moment. Quickly, a mien of forlorn resignation replaced the smile. "Now what? When do the Under Spirits claim me and take me to the Hells?"

"Why would they want you?" asked Sarah.

"Because I killed you all. My soul is damned. Isn't it?"

At this the gathered throng smiled and shook their heads.

Nawizi explained, "You're not damned. We helped save you."

"By haunting me?"

"We didn't haunt you. We called to you letting you know we did not blame you," answered Bonny. "The more you blamed yourself, the harder we tried to reach you."

"Sure seemed like haunting to me. You all seemed so angry," countered Findlah.

"Not angry, just scared and worried for you," explained Sammy. "Didn't you notice that, as you stopped blaming yourself so much, the quieter we became?"

"We weren't angry, dear friend," added Froh. "We feared for your soul's safety. Your self-doubt and self-loathing brought you perilously close to the Under Spirits."

"Well, if I'm not damned, what next?"

"That's up to you. You can stay as a spirit to help another, or you can go with us to the Heavens," advised Alyce.

"The Heavens? What's it like?" Findlah inquired.

The group shrugged. "We don't know, none of us have been there," said Rage. "They stayed here for you."

Findlah began to weep. "Are you sure I'm not damned? I've denied you all paradise!"

Her weeping abruptly stopped, drowned out by raucous, amused laughter.

"Always thought you controlled more than you truly did," chortled Cheye.

"We decided to stay; you did not force us to stay. Our choice. It was always our choice in life and afterwards," he added. "Our task is complete. We will move on. You can choose a task or come with us."

"You've been in my thoughts and dreams for years, decades and centuries; I could not bear to be without you," announced Findlah.

"Let's go!"

Willie's Bad Day
by Robert Richmond

"Good Morning, sir. How may I help you?" requested Willie Bendabracket.

"Just looking at the moment. I've been told you're the Goblin to come to for a mechanical bow."

"Well thank you, thank you. I do try. And if I may be so bold, your information is quite correct. I make the finest mechanical crossbows in PittsBirm. I have a Meker, my brand name, for any situation."

The well-dressed humel began to meander about Willie's shop. Willie gave the customer ten minutes of gawking before approaching him again.

"May I ask what you are looking for?"

"Something for home defense."

"Ah, well. Over here I have the Crew Meker. Perfect for defending keep or manor home. I can and will paint the Meker so it blends in with the décor of your abode. It does require a crew of two to operate this large crossbow, but it will launch a bolt out to five hundred yards, accurately."

"Actually, I was looking for something I might use myself."

"Over here is the Crank Meker. It's the largest single-operator Meker I sell. Granted, it's heavy and slow, but it is accurate out to three hundred and fifty yards. All you'll need is one shot to stop your attacker. The secret is the steel twine cable that you crank into position to shoot."

"I like that, but…. mmm… I don't think the wife would be able to use that if I wasn't home."

"I understand. I understand perfectly. Well then, how about my base model, the Meke? I can make it for you from various fine woods, put on different finishes, etc. It's easy to use, accurate to two hundred and fifty yards and most humelles can use it with a little bit of training. The secret is these oblong wheels at the ends of the arms. They're called cams. They allow for a person with lesser strength to pull back the wire, load, and fire. The cams and such are what make the difference between your standard crossbow and a mechanical bow. Although the names are used interchangeably now, the mechanicals allow for less fatigue and more rapid reloading."

"What about this one? This little one?"

"Oh that? That's the GoMeker. I make that for folks of my stature. The Goblin-sized Meker is just as accurate as the humel-sized. Many humels buy a GoMeker for their children to use. An excellent device for a young hunter in training."

"Do you have anything smaller?"

Warning bells went off in Willie's head. But he had no wish to alienate a possible customer, especially an obviously wealthy potential customer. However, this supposed customer spent ten minutes wandering around the shop, then listened to Willie's entire sales pitch only to ask about a small mechanical bow. Willie suspected this humel shopped for someone rather than something.

"Well, I do make the GoMeker in a size for Goblin children."

"So it would fit in my hand?"

"You could carry it with one hand, but using it would be most difficult and inaccurate. I strongly recommend against you getting one that small. Besides, as you know, the Overlord has banned handheld mechanicals and crossbows. He claims that only thieves, scalawags, and assassins use them."

"True, true, and I wouldn't want to do anything illegal. Well, thank you very much for your time. I'll be back later with the wife."

"Good day, sir." As the customer left the shop Willie stared after him and whispered, "Were you looking or investigating?"

Later that same day as Willie held the door open for his last customer, his friend Riley Knottwise walked in. Ushering his client out, Willie said, "Thank you for your custom, kind sir; I'm sure those Goblin children in WashLon will enjoy their new GoMekers."

"If those are headed for Goblin children, then I'm the Overlord's left buttocks," scoffed Riley.

Willie, laughing, countered with, "Well, you've always been a bit of an ass."

"Don't laugh too hard, Willie. If the Guard ever trace those four handhelds back to you, you could be in real trouble."

As he dropped the Gold Squares into his till, Willie made a rude noise, then waved off his best friend's warning.

"Even if they recognize those as my Mekers, so what? I can honestly say I made them for Goblin children. When the devices left here, no hand grip protruded from any of them."

"Drafter feathers," scowled Riley. "If you didn't intend for a hand grip, then why the dove tailing and the dowel holes? At least you had the good sense to stop stamping the damn things with your 'brand name.'"

"Modifications requested by the customer. I'm not psychic," Willie piously argued. "I've no way of knowing his intentions other than what he told me. And for your information, I stopped labeling my creations because unscrupulous tinkerers were putting out inferior copies and stamping them with my brand in order to garner prices they did not deserve."

"Don't get all haughty with me. And if you keep lying to yourself, it'll be your neck on the block. Especially if you continue with your other mechanical endeavors. I'll stick with my Ironsmithing. Much safer."

"I have no idea what you're talking about," rejoined Willie as his long-nailed fingers brushed his long eyebrows back into shape.

"Feigning innocence with me isn't going to work, I supply the parts, remember? Your little mechanical lock picking contraption isn't being used by the Guard to rescue trapped folks in locked rooms now, is it?"

"I can only assume it's being used for legal purposes," Willie countered loftily before inquiring, "And speaking of your Ironsmithing… when do I get my gears, cams and wheels?"

"When I'm damn good and ready, not before," blustered Riley. With a wink, he added, "Or next Unusday, whichever is first."

"Good. I've got customers waiting. Now get out of here so I can lock up. I've got dinner waiting now."

"See you tomorrow, and remember what I said," admonished Riley. He gave a quick wave to his friend.

Because of his wave, Riley did not see the humelle entering Willie's shop. He bumped rather forcefully into her legs.

"Pardon me," he exclaimed as he bowed away from the stranger. Something didn't feel right about her. Riley took two steps and realized what was wrong. Hardened muscle hid under that middle class dress, not the soft flesh one expected from a humelle who spends her days indoors.

"How may I help you?" queried Willie as the humelle entered his shop.

"I'm told you're the Goblin that makes Mekers, the best mechanical bows money can buy."

"I'm flattered; I don't know if they're the best, but I do try." Willie mentally arranged his standard sales pitch and solicitously began with, "Are you looking for a gift for a friend?"

"For a friend? Why not for myself?" she interrupted.

"Pardon; I did not mean to insult. It's just that ladies such as yourself rarely use weapons."

The humelle chuckled. At that same moment at his front door, a wide-eyed Riley pointed at this new customer and mouthed the word 'Guard'. Riley then ran. Willie's sales pitch slid out of his brain and slithered down icy, fear-chilled vertebrae.

"You'd be surprised what a 'lady' such as myself uses. Now, the four handheld *Mekers* you just sold have been confiscated. The humel who purchased them is under arrest and soon will be a head shorter. In an effort to save himself he's going to start talking, beginning with where he purchased those little wonders. When he does, you shall keep him company on the scaffold."

"I didn't-"

"Don't deny." The humelle interrupted Willie's denial with a quick slash of her hand. "It's too late. You must choose between two options. One, stay here and accept the consequences of your actions; or two, come with me now and possibly avoid that fatal cut. I might add, you don't have a lot of time to decide."

Quickly, Willie made his choice. He opted for the dubious survival offered by this strange humelle. Rapidly emptying his till, and the small safe in the back, the terrified Goblin followed the humelle through the streets of PittsBirm. She moved decisively. She knew the town and its alleyways. With every pause to look around a building corner, Willie's pores dripped more and more fear. A shout behind him had his heart threatening to beat out of his throat. Only after several gulps and a frantic glance did Willie realize that the shout had been two friends meeting. Not long after, another shout, this time a loud 'hey,' nearly caused Willie to soil his pants.

Eventually, Willie and his unnamed rescuer rode through woods. Now that his fear adrenaline drained out of his terror-packed brain, Willie evaluated his circumstances and his companion. He rode on a Goblin-bred mount, not easy for a humelle to come by. The pony stood waiting for him, next to the mount she now rode. The humelle herself had flashed some leg - leather-clad legs under that middle class dress. She rode astride her horse through the woods with confidence. Her hair was sun-touched, as was her skin. This, again, was unusual for a middle class humelle who spent most of her time indoors. Their dash through town had been fast and precise without any panic on her part. Any attempt at conversation had been met with a "shh" and a glare or she simply ignored him. She communicated her wishes and directions by grunts and the pointing of fingers or the waving of hands.

The pair rode until each tree's shadow combined with its neighbor to darken the forest, even though the sun still shone. Willie suddenly smelled wood smoke. Now alert to a fire, he spotted the campsite and their apparent destination. Upon entering the camp, Willie's initially thought ruffians and brigands. Then, he looked closer. Although each humel and Dwarf wore mismatched armor and weapons, everyone and everything appeared neat and clean. The camp's stools and tents stood symmetrically around the campfire. No booze! Willie saw no one imbibing. This was highly unusual, indeed. Willie gazed around confusedly; his brain identified details, but comprehension remained elusive. A light push from his rescuer and Willie stumbled towards one of the tents.

"Why is it that nothing is as it seems?" Willie muttered.

"'Bout time you got here," a Sylvan said as he lightly and soundlessly dropped from a tree behind Willie, either oblivious to or ignoring Willie's concern.

"Short l..," The rest of her response garbled as she shucked off her disguise. The middle-class house wife disappeared to reveal a svelte warrior clad in leather with a large dagger on her right hip and another dagger in her left boot.

"An encampment of tidy 'criminals' composed of Dwarves, humels, and a Sylvan?" Willie muttered to himself.

"He's here," she announced. To Willie's question she replied, "We're not criminals, deary, just misunderstood."

"Oops, I didn't realize that was aloud," Willie sheepishly admitted. Any retort the humelle would have made was cut off by a voice and humel emerging from the nearby tent.

"Excellent; we can now get things rolling," a familiar voice announced. Exiting from the tent was his last customer - the arrested customer. The one with the handhelds! The humel heading to be beheaded!

"What in the hells below is going on?" demanded Willie.

"You've been recruited by the Hounds of the Hunt," announced the humel as he straightened and walked over to Willie.

"Recruited? Who? What?"

"Have a seat, and I'll explain."

Willie plopped down in the nearest camp stool. His female escort wandered off and began a conversation with the Sylvan.

"My name is Everett Hydeswell. The Hounds of the Hunt, or simply 'Hounds' as we call ourselves, is a mercenary group comprised of former Overlord's Guards and other like-minded individuals. Our sole employer is the Overlord."

"Huh? Why would the Overlord need mercenaries when he has the Guard?"

"There are times and situations where the Overlord cannot be seen as acting directly. The phrase is plausible deniability. We must be discreet, observant, and sober at all times."

"Ooohhh. So if things go bad, you get thrown under the drafter cart and the Overlord claims innocence."

"You catch on quickly, Willie."

"So why me? And what, just for the sake of argument, if I say no?"

"You have a skill set we need for a particular operation." Everett smiled, the smile of the cat looking at its next mouse meal. "Should you say no, your last sale comes to the attention of the Guard via a tearful confession from a distraught humel with a change of heart."

Willie glared at Everett. "In other words, I work with you or I get my head lopped off."

"As I said, you catch on quickly."

"But other Goblins have the same skills I have," Willie protested. "Why single me out?"

"Your hands aren't clean... not quite dirty. Let's just say you have enough dirt under your nails to allow us the opportunity to make you this offer."

"Offer, my ass! It's blackmail," retorted Willie.

"Call it what you will. I call it effective recruiting."

"So what do I have to do?"

"Nothing too arduous or dangerous. Just travel with a fellow Hound to Lost Ways and--"

"Lost Ways? The Overlord cleared that place out two centuries ago. His 'audit' of the place is legendary. According to the stories I've heard, the executioner had to buy a new ax, and then he had to turn around and replace that one. Not a single city employee survived."

Everett laughed and shook his head. "Considerable exaggeration. While there were a number of fatalities, most of the city's government survived. Back to your question. Your expertise is needed in Lost Ways. We've come across a number of mechanical bows, which are unusual, along with some other mechanical devices that have 'unique' properties. We would like for you to help us track down the creators of these items."

"That's it?"

"That's it. Nothing dangerous at all; just your opinion on the items."

"Sounds deceptively simple," Willie agreed suspiciously.

"Good. We have a tent set up for you. Go ahead and kip out. You'll start to Lost Ways in the morning."

Everett got up and re-entered his tent. Willie's escort, seeing Everett rise, walked over to guide him to his tent. The Hounds planned well; everything in the tent fit Willie's diminutive Goblin size. After using the small hand towel to wipe away the last vestiges of fear sweat from his bald head, Willie rummaged through the backpack. It contained everything a Goblin could want for a long distance trip. To his horror, one of his own GoMekers stood in the corner with a quiver of bolts. He remembered he sold this GoMeker to a Goblin hunter passing through PittsBirm on his way south. That Goblin had stopped by over two months before! The Hounds had known about him for that long?! Eventually, Willie's worry receded with the realization the Guard never arrested him. Willie went to sleep that night wondering about his shop and who his new companion would be.

Willie awoke to cussing. Eventually, the cussing stopped but the anger and volume remained unchanged.

"Spirits Above, Everett! Just shoot me! Put a dagger through my eye! At least kill me quickly! You want me going to Lost Ways with a Goblin towner? If I'm lucky he'll be dead in a week. If I'm not he'll be dead in a week and he'll get me killed too! Whatever made you think-"

"Relax, I'm not trying to kill you." Everett attempted to calm his angry friend. "Yes, he's a towner, but I think he'll survive the trip and be a most helpful asset, Fuil."

"Bah! Have you at least seen him drink?"

"No, why?"

"Because, ya' soft in the head, humel, the places we'll frequent in Lost Ways… oh why worry. We'll all be dead before we get there anyway."

Peeking out of his tent, Willie spotted the Dwarf making all the noise immediately. The Dwarf staring belligerently up at Everett seemed to have been pulled straight out of the encyclopedia. He was clad in chain mail, with a shield on his back. The ebony-headed Dwarf's beard had been trimmed short. An ax hung from one hip, but a curiously small red hammer dangled from the other. The Dwarf's pony stood complacently behind its master, ignoring his tirade. A crossbow hung from the saddle's pommel, and the feathered bolt shafts could be seen peeking up from the other side of the mount.

"Here. I'll turn my back. Put the dagger through my heart and be quick," snarled the Dwarf as he turned from Everett. In doing so, he spotted Willie. "Spirits Above! There it is! Damnation, Everett, couldn't you at least grab a green-skinned runt with some heft to it? Dying because of that scrawny thing's gonna keep me out of paradise for sure!"

Two stomping struts later, the Dwarf mounted his steed and galloped off.

"Oh good. You're awake and you've seen your new partner. I'm sure the two of you will get along well," beamed Everett with all of the sincerity of a used-horse dealer.

"I thought you said Hounds had to be sober all the time? If that's the case, why is my ability to drink being questioned by that Dwarf?" a skeptical Willie demanded.

"There are times when drinking is necessary to blend in with the crowd; even then a Hound must be able to consume enough to be part of the group, but still keep his wits about him," responded Everett.

Willie, with some help, packed his tent and backpack and mounted his pony. Everett walked him along a game trail for about an hour. At a small stream sat a very disgruntled Dwarf.

"Fuil Innen, meet Willie Bendabracket. Willie, this is Fuil. He'll be your guide, escort, and fellow investigator. Good hunting, my fellow Hounds."

"Yeah, up yours, Everett," grumbled Fuil.

"Well met, Fuil. I do hope our partnership proves mutually beneficial."

"I am so cursed, a Goblin towner and a con artist at that." Fuil muttered to the sky. "What's so special about you that I've got to risk my ass carrying you all the way to Lost Ways?"

"Everett seems to think that my skills are needed in tracking down certain items you Hounds have found."

"Oh, you're the contraption maker. Alright, here's how it goes. You do what I say when I say it. When it comes to a fight, don't get in my way. Anything else, just don't get in my way."

The trip to Lost Ways took four extraordinary months for Willie. Having been born and raised in PittsBirm, Willie's knowledge of the wilderness came from books and stories. Fuil Innean proved to be a marginal teacher and terrible companion. A short temper, combined with an obvious dislike for his assignment, made traveling with Fuil unpleasant. Fuil cussed everything Willie did. Willie took too long to set up his tent, took too long to pack it up, pooped too close to camp, drank Gutfire like a child, puked loud enough to wake a dragon - the list seemed endless. Willie's only satisfaction came with the realization as they rode through the gates of Lost Ways that Fuil hadn't had anything to cuss or fuss about that morning.

The pair took up residence in a rather seedy tavern and inn. Two days later, Willie and Fuil met with a couple of fellow Hounds.

"Alright, runt. Tell me what you can about these," demanded Fuil.

Willie looked at the two boxes and the small mechanical bow dubiously. Picking up the tools Fuil had provided, Willie began deconstructing the bow first.

"Well, I can tell you this. It's not Goblin- or Dwarf-made…"

"We know that. Hurry it up," snarled Fuil.

"Patience, Fuil. Let the Goblin do his work," countered one of the Hounds. Willie couldn't remember the slightly plump humelle's name.

With a nod of thanks to his defender, Willie continued: "Not Goblin- or Dwarf-made; I don't know enough about Troll work to make an opinion. However, what I can say is that whoever made this is skilled but doesn't want to show it. Look here. See how these fit together? Originally, the join was well done; yet, the builder went back and messed about to make it look less perfect on casual inspection."

"Why would anyone do that?" queried the other Hound, a pox-scarred humel. "Why cheapen your work? Make it appear less?"

"Good question. No idea. Let me finish, please."

Willie finished with the mechanical bow and began his disassembly of the boxes.

"Okay, the obvious first," Willie started with a nod at the glowering Fuil. "I've no idea who made these. They're obviously lock boxes with needle traps for any unwary thief. Once again, created by at least a master crafter, yet he or she has disguised the quality of the work making the boxes appear less capable than they are. Whoever made these is going to a lot of trouble to appear barely competent; yet their work is superb. The metal in some of these components is strange to me."

"That's why you're here, Fuil," announced the humelle.

"Hrrmpf, like I'm really needed."

"Go ahead, tell us what this gear is made of then," she challenged.

Fuil picked up the small gear, stared at if for a moment then sang a low tune. Nothing happened.

"Well, don't take all day," pestered the humel, grinning at the startled look on Fuil's face.

Willie stared at the group, completely oblivious to the significance of Fuil's now flummoxed expression and the goading from his companion. Then Fuil grabbed one of Willie's tools, a thin steel probe. Singing the same low tune, Fuil concentrated on the probe. It began to melt, then to twist and bend. Willie watched, amazed, as the probe began to dance in the Dwarf's hand.

"Okay, Silver Singer, so what is it with that gear?" the humelle demanded.

"I've no idea," answered Fuil as he placed the twisted probe back on the table and picked up the gear. Frowning, Fuil sang a number of different tunes, each with the same non response from the gear. As Fuil sang his tunes, Willie turned to the humelle and asked a question.

"What's a Silver Singer?"

"A Dwarf who can sing to metal. A Singer can sing and easily manipulate the base metals. A Silver Singer, like our friend here, is even more special. He can do the same with base and precious metals. Because of this, with a song or two a *competent* Silver Singer can identify any metal on this world. It's not a talent Dwarves like to talk about."

"I got your competent, you sassy wench," grouched Fuil. "This ain't from here."

"Huh? What do you mean?" The startled humelle turned to her glowering companion.

"What I'm saying is that this metal ain't from here, it didn't come from Gaia."

"A star metal?" Bewildered and pensive, Willie picked up the gear. "If what you say is true, then this really doesn't make any sense. Why use such rare and valuable metal to make junk with it?"

"Indeed, that's why we asked for help with this," said the humel. "These devices and that mechanical have been involved with some unusual deaths and occurrences. We need you two to track down the source."

Weeks of tracking whispers, rumors, tall tales, deaths, robberies and a few more boxes led Willie and Fuil into the sewers of Lost Ways. The last three devices Willie took apart all had small bits of sewer filth stuck somewhere in the gearing. Now, Willie stood knee deep in body waste, with Fuil Innean. For several days now, Willie slithered and sneaked through the sewers of Lost Ways. He cursed Everett. He cursed Fuil. He even cursed Riley for not warning him earlier. Most of all, Willie cursed himself. Willie understood why he was here and he understood the reason for Fuil. Fuil had been chosen for this mission because of his Singing ability; just as Willie had been selected for his ability with mechanical devices.

"The only thing fouler than the sewers is Fuil's temper," Willie mused to himself. Each day of fruitless searching brought on more vulgarities and threats to Willie's wellbeing. Fuil's sudden raised fist brought Willie to a stop. Willie looked ahead, straining to see what had alarmed the Dwarf. Since both Willie and Fuil possessed night sight, they did not carry torches with them. This may have saved their lives.

Up ahead of them, laying low in the sewage, a creature lurked with its head and nostrils just above the water line. The creature's demeanor indicated Willie and Fuil remained undetected. Behind and above the creature in the sewer wall, Willie saw the faint outline of a doorframe. Fuil slowly raised his crossbow. A quick succession of thumps left the creature floating in the offal. Willie slipped past the Ogre. Fuil's bolt feather was buried deep in its forehead. It had been hiding in a sewage-filled hole deep enough to conceal the creature. At the door, Fuil sang a low hushed tune. Willie saw the metal latch flair brightly, then watched as the slag slid to the floor. Motioning Willie to one side of the doorway, Fuil took up a position on the opposite side. Using his ax, Fuil pushed open the latchless door. Whispering, hissing things flashed out into the sewer and ricocheted off the walls before plopping into the miasma of filth.

Fuil reloaded his crossbow and, after a quick glance, scuttled through the now open doorway. After a quick prayer to the Spirits above, Willie followed.

They scurried through the passageway until they reached another door. Fuil opened it as he had done with the first door, but this one was not trapped. Once through this door, Willie could smell the acrid odors of a forge. Fuil now acted as a four-legged hound, following his nose to the forge and the source of the unusual mechanicals. Willie could see they were close; the walls of the hallway they entered shone with the reflected heat of the forge. Suddenly a door opened and two trolls with two Goblins emerged and immediately attacked Willie and Fuil. Willie downed one with his GoMeker. Fuil's ax and crossbow accounted for the others.

"Too easy," mumbled Fuil.

"What?"

"Too easy. They died too easy; they didn't fight as they should. I don't like it," muttered Fuil.

"I'm perfectly happy with their ineptitude," commented Willie as he and Fuil reloaded. "Let's keep going and hope everyone else is just as incompetent."

The two Hounds approached the door from which their attackers had emerged and peered inside. They had found the workplace; now to find the one responsible.

"I wonder-" Willie had started to say when an unseen door opened and a tall humel walked into the shop.

"Ah, so nice to see you. Injured? No? Good. I'm pleased."

"Who are you?" blurted Willie.

"Why I'm you." The humel declared. His eyes reflected an odd violet sheen.

"A Doppelganger Demon!" bellowed Fuil as he fired his crossbow. "Shoot! Run! We can't fight it!"

The bolt's flesh shearing thwack coincided with the shattering crash of Fuil's weapon as Fuil fired and fled. The bolt struck the humel in the neck, which caused his head to rock back. The wound should have dropped the humel to the floor, as his trachea, esophagus and spinal cord were severed.

Fuil, running? Fuil the fearless? The Dwarf never ran from a fight during their entire trip to Lost Ways. He fired his bolt and ran! What did he yell? What demon? Confusion paralyzed Willie.

Willie watched, horrified, as the smiling humel slowly pulled the bolt out of his neck and tossed the missile to the floor. Fuil's desperate splashing became fainter and fainter.

"I require your knowledge and, more importantly, your face," the demon explained as his neck wound healed. "It's why I fashioned those mechanical bows and things with their little fake flaws. Then, I made sure those fool Hounds found them. Having discovered my little treasures, I made sure your name soon floated about. I knew they would bring you to me."

Suddenly a foursome of tendrils lashed out and bound the mesmerized Willie. "I would have liked the pair of you; the Dwarf would have been a nice bonus," the demon continued. "Unfortunately, he did the only smart thing he could. He ran."

Two of the binding tendrils began snaking towards Willie's ears.

An hour later, Willie, throat a little sore from the screaming, skipped out of the sewers bouncing a scrap of Abyss Iron in his hand.

"Now, then," he said to no one in particular, "where to start, where to start? Ah. I know… Riley. He still owes me those gears and such. So I think that's a good place to start. Home."

A small pop sounded as air rushed in to fill the space once occupied by Willie, not a Bendabraket.

About the Author

Robert is a new author and an old Nuclear Medicine Technologist. Gaiahexnonahept began to emerge just a couple of years ago as an oasis from the realities of working at the regional trauma center. Living in Memphis, Tennessee for over twenty years, he is surrounded by dogs, cats and humans. Two of his favorite humans are his wife, Alyce and his daughter Sarah. Nessy and Sam, the resident English Springer Spaniels, are a wonderful audience for tales about Gaiahexnonahept. The cats could care less.

---

i

Printed in Great
Britain
by Amazon